The Old Roseans

The Old Roseans

A Story of Atonement

D. Van Buren

Based on a television pilot of the same name.

MOUNTAIN ARBOR
PRESS

MOUNTAIN ARBOR
PRESS *an Imprint of BookLogix*
Alpharetta, GA

ISBN: 978-1-6653-0214-2 - Paperback
eISBN: 978-1-6653-0215-9 - ePub

Printed in the United States of America   0 1 1 3 2 1

♾ This paper meets the requirements of ANSI/NISO Z39.48-1992 (Permanence of Paper)

For my grandfather Benjamin Harley Jr., great-grandfather Benjamin "Papa" Harley Sr., great-grandmother Vina Van Buren, grandmother Naomi Williams, grandmother Eslynne Downes, aunt Arkansas Houston, aunt Leah Harley, uncle Robert Harley, aunt Hattie Harley, aunt Helen Harley, aunt Ellen Harley-Anderson, aunt Minnie Harley-Flint, aunt Geraldine Harley-Taylor, aunt Marie Harley-Grant, aunt Frances Chance, uncle John Chance, my sister Kimberly McCullough, my cousin Maxine Baker, Ms. Bernice, Mr. David House, Ms. Carol Harris, Mr. Joseph Rigby, Mr. Leroy Cummings, Mr. Wellington Pitts, Mr. Anthony "Tony" Ray, Mobile, Alabama football head coach Butch, US Army JROTC Master Sergeant Walter Ray Pollock, and my hero Michael Vieira.

Last but not least, to my dearest mother, Vina Harley. Despite only being given four years with you, they were the very best times of my life. I've been told I often act like you. I certainly look just like you. There are no words to describe how much I miss and love you. I am forever and always your pride and joy.

Your loving son,
—D. Van Buren

On July 17, 1998, for the first time in history, over one hundred sovereign states backed a treaty-based statute that created the International Criminal Court. From that date on, it was referred to as "The Rome Statute."

Recognizing that such grave crimes threaten the peace, security, and well-being of the world, the most serious crimes of concern to the international community must not go unpunished . . .

—Preamble to the Rome Statute of the International Criminal Court

Contents

Author's Note

The outcome of the Armistice at the eleventh hour on the eleventh day of November in 1918 led me to create an original television pilot for a multiple-season TV series. This mystery thriller is based on that pilot. The pilot's teaser—introduced before chapter one—is the only part of the book written in teleplay format. Writing this story with an ensemble cast was one of my more demanding lessons won. Hence, it is with great pleasure that I present: The Old Roseans (Les Anciens Roséens).

D. Van Buren

Ensemble Cast

Adad Osman Efendi:
Adad is an International Criminal Court deputy prosecutor. The forty-something widower is an Ottoman prince by right of birth.

Alexander Osman Efendi:
Alexander is a teenage Ottoman prince by right of birth.

Amorette Samusenko:
Amorette is a Russian Space Forces captain. She is in her thirties and unmarried.

Andrea Hartmann:
Andrea is the executive director of European Union Aviation Safety. She is in her fifties and married.

Benjamin Spelman Rockefeller:
Ben, in his fifties and married, is president of the United States. He is also a descendant of the late American oil tycoon, John Davison Rockefeller Sr.

Britta Warburg:
Britta, in her forties and married, is a Jewish Canadian Supreme Court senior puisne justice.

Catherine Victoria Romanov of Prussia:
Catherine is an unmarried flight surgeon with the US Air

Force Special Operations Command. She is in her late twenties and a princess of Germany and Russia by right of birth.

Christopher David Kawānanakoa:

Christopher, in his forties and married, is the US secretary of state. He is also heir to the Hawaiian monarchy's throne by right of birth.

Colonel Xavier Gevargese:

Xavier is the twenty-fifth Special Mission Forces Division commander (Syrian Tiger Forces). He is in his forties and married.

Donnie Nowak:

Donnie is the chief justice on the nine-member Canadian Supreme Court. He is in his forties and married.

Dhruva Jin Aisin Gioro:

Dhruva, known as DJ, is a US Secret Service special agent. The unassuming African American-Taiwanese claimant to the Dragon Throne—the monarch of China's throne—is in her twenties.

Edith Augusta Marie of Prussia:

Edith, a former East German intelligence officer, is the investigatory powers commissioner for the United Kingdom. She is a princess of Germany by right of birth, in her sixties, and estranged from her husband.

General Sahib Gevargese:

Sahib is the minister of defense for all Syrian Arab Armed Forces. He is in his seventies and married.

General Sheldon Whitney Straight:

Sheldon is the US Central Command commander. He is in his forties, married, and an expert in Russian and Mandarin Chinese. Michael Whitney Straight, his late grandfather, was a KGB spy.

General Zahid Ahmadi:

Zahid is a senior Air Force Intelligence Directorate officer. He is in his forties and married.

Gerard de Gaulle:

Gerard is the chairman and managing director of the International Monetary Fund. He is in his thirties and un-married.

James Joyce:

James (known as JJ), of Cuban and Seminole Native American descent, is the director of National Intelligence. He is in his forties and single.

Judy Foster:

Judy is the US ambassador for the United Nations. The Pulitzer Prize winning author is in her forties and married.

Jin Aisin Gioro:

In his sixties and married, Jin (known as Martin) is a re-tired Taiwanese American politician. Martin is also a descendant of Puyi, the last emperor of China.

Kirsten Oppiehiem:

Kirsten, an archeologist and divorcée in her sixties, is a

retired German banker and lawyer. She is also a former East German intelligence officer.

Leah Oppiehiem de Rothschild:
Leah is a teenage heir to two European banking dynasties.

Mahdi Hamanti:
Mahdi is a Syrian army captain. He is in his thirties and unmarried.

Mark Lamont:
Mark, British ambassador to the United States, is a world-renowned historian. He is in his forties, married, and a descendant of American banker, Thomas Lamont.

Maximilian von Habsburg:
Maximilian is informally titled as an Imperial and Royal Archduke of Austria. He is in his early-twenties and unmarried.

Michael Phillips:
Michael, sixteenth in the line of succession to the British throne, is an unmarried thirty-something British military commander, and European Space Agency astronaut candidate.

Nadia Turhan Efendi:
Nadia is a teenage Ottoman princess by right of birth.

Nicholas Romanov III of Russia:
Nicholas, a former KGB officer assigned to Berlin in the seventies and eighties for counterintelligence operations

against NATO-aligned countries, is the Russian Federation defense minister in command of all Russian armed forces. The sixty-something, Russian prince—by right of birth—is estranged from his wife.

Nina Maczek:
Nina is the governor general of Canada. She is in her late-twenties and unmarried.

Paul Berenberg-Gossler:
Paul, in his forties and divorced, is the US secretary of defense. He is also a descendant of the brothers Hans and Paul Berenberg, founders of the world's oldest surviving merchant bank.

Pasha Pavlichenko:
Pasha is a British metropolitan police officer assigned to the British Royalty and Specialist Protection Command. He is in his thirties and married.

Patrick de Rothschild:
In his fifties and married, Patrick is the peacetime commander in chief of all unified German armed forces. He also is one of the leaders of a European banking dynasty.

Robert Ethan Albion:
Robert, in his sixties and married, is vice president of the United States. He is also the descendant of an American slave who became a British Colonial Marine during the War of 1812.

Rudolf von Habsburg:
Rudolf is in his sixties and widowed. His ancestral title is Imperial Highness Archduke of Austria.

Sebastian Hartmann:
Sebastian is a European Space Agency astronaut candidate. He is in his thirties, unmarried, and in command of Germany's largest armed forces battalion.

Salah El Sayed:
Salah is a Syrian army lieutenant colonel. He is in his sixties and widowed.

Thomas Arthur:
Thomas is the secretary to the governor general of Canada. He is in his sixties and married.

Vice Admiral Gabriel Kolchak:
Gabriel is the Russian Federation's Main Military Medical Directorate's commander. There are rumors that the fifty-something physician and widower has royal Russian blood flowing through his veins.

Vina da Costa Greene:
In her fifties and married, Vina is the assistant to the president of the United States for the Department of National Security Affairs. Her biological great-grandfathers are Richard Theodore Greener—the first African American graduate of Harvard College—and American banking tycoon, John Pierpont Morgan.

Vincent Bunche:

Vincent, the Central Intelligence Agency director and expert in the Arabic language and culture, is single and in his forties. His grandfather, Ralph Bunche, is the first African American recipient of the Nobel Prize.

Preamble

Le Rosey is a private boarding school near Lake Geneva in Rolle, Switzerland. Since its 1880 founding at the fourteenth-century Château du Rosey, the school has become one of the most prestigious academic institutes known worldwide.

Against a backdrop that flawlessly envelopes the wondrous beauty and magnificence of the Swiss Alps, this story trails the extraordinary lives of a group of former Le Rosey classmates.

They are affectionately known as Old Roseans (Anciens Roséens). Their intricate world, riddled with bonds and profoundly ingrained deception, carries dark secrets. One that could destroy them all involves an individual the International Criminal Court wants for horrific war crimes.

The Old Roseans
Les Anciens Roséens

TEASER

EXT. MATTITUCK INLET — MATTITUCK, NEW YORK — DAWN

From the channel's sandy edges. We see—

A FABULOUS WATERWAY

EXT. MATT-a-MAR MARINA — DAWN

A legendary motel, boat ramps, dock, and on-premise catering? No problem! This is why recreational boaters come here!

We are in the TOWN OF SOUTHOLD. It's part of one village and ten hamlets. On top of that The weather isn't good; it's perfect!

EXT. MATT-a-MAR MARINA'S MAIN HOUSE — DAWN

Erected in 1965. On nine-acres. Brick constructed. Three levels. Countless memories that include—

A HIDDEN OFFICE

INT. OFFICE — CONTINUOUS

The office is soundproof. Air purifying plants. No windows. Not to mention—

VINA DA COSTA GREENE

The lovely middle-aged U.S. Secret Service protectee wearing her husband's blue and white pinstriped pajamas is seated behind an oak wood desk.

Grey numbers and lettering over a white b.g.
that READS: 05:57 a.m. is visible on the-

DESK TELEPHONE

Hopefully. This time. Good news.

                    VINA
            (Mouth near the phone's
             speaker.)
        Did they make it to Aleppo?

                MALE'S VOICE (O.S.)
                (Almost inaudibly)
        Yes.

                    VINA
                (Anxious)
        Are they still alive?

SUDDENLY —

Satellite communication is cut off.

EXT. DESERT HIGHWAY — SYRIA — MORNING

ROCKS. Not just on both sides of the highway.
They're all over the place. No vegetation. Heat
is incomprehensible.

We're near the forgotten cities of Stylites,
Serjilla, and Albara. It does not rain here.
This is a zone of absolute silence. We cannot
be on Earth. But. We are!

Then. The SOUND of a motor vehicle.

EXT. THREE-DOOR LADA OKA HATCHBACK — MOMENTS LATER

We see a midnight blue 1970s Soviet Union
designed automobile traveling on the highway.
Its accelerating . . .

. . . FAST!

INT. HATCHBACK — CONTINOUS (MOVING)

A MAN AND WOMAN

Both good-looking. In their late twenties. The man is decked out in a dark grey suit. A white scarf is draped around his head.

A black hijab covers the woman's head. A long black shirt covers everything else below her shoulders.

THE CHAUFFEUR

A teenager dressed in a white linen garment. Blue jeans. Basketball sneakers. He just lit another cigarette.

                    CHAUFFEUR
          (To passengers in Arabic
           with subtitles)
     If you're thinking about closing your
     eyes. This would be a good time.

While the blue hatchback crosses a dry river bed. The chauffeur exhales smoke. His PASSENGERS lean back.

However . . .

. . . they don't close their eyes.

INT. SOUQ AL-ATTARINE — ALEPPO, SYRIA — AFTERNOON

A densely populated marketplace. It's the finest place in the world for perfume, cologne, spice, and exotic raw meat.

We recognize someone. A passenger from the hatchback.

OUR MAN IN THE DARK GREY SUIT

He's smelling a fragrance on his wrist near —

FOUR PLAINLY DRESSED MEN

As THREE MEN, thirties, provide close protection. The FOURTH MAN, sixties, sniffs cinnamon and nutmeg.

> FOURTH MAN
> (To Grey Suit Man in
> Arabic with subtitles)
> Who sent you?

> GREY SUIT MAN
> The United Nations.

> FOURTH MAN (PRE-LAP)
> What do they want?

SLOW MOTION: Grey Suit Man lifts a subcompact pistol to eye level.

> FADE TO BLACK.

> GREY SUIT MAN (O.S.)
> Atonement . . .

END OF TEASER

TV PILOT EPISODE 101

"The Hunt for an Elusive Individual Begins."

Chapter One
Wengen

2015

*T*he lifeblood of Wengen, a mountainous village found in central Switzerland, is Wengen Railway Station. It's also where a supersonic boom had just forced everyone within earshot to look up. After four lightweight fighter jets from the Swiss Air Force aerobatic team flew beyond eyesight, Rudolf von Habsburg and Sebastian Hartmann briefly relived the memory of time no more.

"I remember now," Rudolf said while standing with his head held high in the heart of the Swiss Alps. "Many guests were gathered for the commemorative service at the parade grounds that connect the Bendlerblock with the Bundeswehr Memorial for Colonel Claus von Stauffenberg. And you were at the head of the Wachbataillon when I saw you . . ."

"When you saw me cry," Sebastian, clothed in a grey mountaineering parka, finished as they spoke German.

"Everyone shed tears that day," Rudolf acknowledged

with gloved hands that filled his dark-brown, wool overcoat's outer pockets. "What was yours for?"

"For the Nazi resistance fighters that were executed," Sebastian answered.

"My tears were for their failure to assassinate Hitler," added Rudolf. "Despite that, I'm grateful for Germany's reunification as well as for the good company of a fellow Old Rosean."

"Thank you," Sebastian proudly replied, following a firm handshake. "By the same token, it's been an enjoyable experience spending time with the head of the House of Habsburg-Lorraine."

At that moment, everything remembered about Berlin in July of 1944 seemed forgotten amid the shaking passing beneath their feet as the next commuter train arrived on time at Wengen Railway Station. While Edith, Patrick, and his teenage daughter Leah left one passenger car. And different tourists poured out of other railroad cars attached to the same yellow-and-green train. Rudolf, Sebastian, and one of the most bitter temperatures recorded in the canton of Bern awaited them.

"I've missed you," Rudolf said with a smile.

"I've missed you too," Edith, covered in her Prussian-blue down jacket, replied as she faced Sebastian. "I trust my cousin wasn't a total bore."

"Only slightly," Sebastian wisecracked.

"I should have known the kindness wouldn't last," said Rudolf as he shook his head.

"I just needed to be convinced you weren't too

preoccupied with your own thoughts to talk to anyone," Edith jokingly replied while Rudolf smirked.

"Did Uncle Rudolf and my brother really not speak on the railway platform?" Leah inquired while she and Patrick, outfitted in identical orange mountaineering down jackets, hugged Sebastian.

"Edith and I have teased one another with exaggerations since . . ."

"The third grade," Edith supplied.

"Weren't the three of you in the same class?" Sebastian asked his stepfather and Leah noticed Rudolf and Edith trading mischievous smiles.

"At that time, Rudolf, Nicholas, Gabriel, and I were on the boys' side of 'the Juniors' campus," Patrick answered Sebastian while they all began to move away from the train. "Kirsten and Edith were on the girls' side. That was when I learned Wengen is a place like no other."

"Because of the Lauberhorn ski races?" asked Leah.

"That's one reason," replied Patrick.

"What's another one?"

"Pure air," interjected the voice of a distinguished young man touring the platform that had just been covered by a blanket of bright white snow. When he approached them with several Wengen Railway Station employees, the group stopped walking.

"Who are you?" asked Leah after taking a second look at the handsome, tall male with dark hair.

"My name is Maximilian von Habsburg VI," he replied. "I'm the acting Wengen Railway Station Manager and

Rudolf's son. But make no mistake; at the same time, local residents will tell you the sacrifice of roads and automobiles isn't easy, they'll also say the trade-off for the pure mountain air is worth the inconvenience."

"I bet she didn't hear a word he said," Edith remarked with a smirk.

"I know she didn't," said Sebastian as he shook his head.

"Are you OK?" Patrick asked Leah.

"Yes, Father."

"Are you also, OK?" Rudolf asked Maximilian.

"Yes, Father," he answered, all the while he kept his eyes fixed on Leah.

"I've never seen Leah so quiet," said Patrick and everyone apart from Maximilian and Leah erupted into laughter.

"I acted the same way," Edith voiced as a gesture of solidarity with Leah.

"The first time you saw my godfather's face?"

"Yes."

"Was Uncle Nicholas as cute as Maximilian is now?" Leah, inspired by the similarities, eagerly asked in a whisper.

"Absolutely."

"Do you have pictures?"

"At Hohenzollern Castle," Edith told her. "Our school yearbook pictures, and wedding portraits are kept in the same chamber as the Crown of His Royal Highness Wilhelm II."

"My apologies for eavesdropping," said Maximilian as he cut into the conversation. "But I remember visiting the Hohenzollern castle with my parents."

"His mother Sophia and I were married in Saint Michael's

chapel at the Castle," inserted Rudolf upon hearing his son bring it up. "The castle also has George Washington and Baron von Steuben's private correspondence."

As Rudolf turned to Maximilian, he tried but couldn't stop himself from tearing up.

"I'm sorry," Rudolf said to him. "But speaking about your mother made me think about our wedding and how much I miss her."

"There's no need to apologize, Papa," said Maximilian while rubbing his father's shoulder. "We both miss her. But I think we should continue to walk as we talk."

"Where is this castle?" Leah inquired very quietly to protect Rudolf from being reminded of his wife and the pain it caused him.

"Near Black Forest National Park and the Swabian Alps of Baden-Württemberg, Germany," answered Edith in a low voice of her own as they strolled unhurriedly. "You have an open invitation."

"Now I know my first stop after graduation," Leah told Edith, who reacted with a sunny smile.

"What school are you in?" asked Maximilian.

"Le Rosey."

"I attended Le Rosey," he replied, kind of surprised.

"I know," she said.

"I don't remember you."

"Because I was twelve at the same time you were sixteen," Leah explained. "Now I'm sixteen."

"That means you're a senior?"

"It does," she answered. "I graduate in June."

"Which academic track did you choose?" inquired Maximilian while thinking how cool Leah seemed to be.

"The French Baccalaureate track was my initial consideration," she answered. "However, by the end of class two, I had decided the International Baccalaureate track was better for me."

"I chose the same track," he said, thrilled about what they shared in common.

"No, you didn't."

"But I did," he swore as they chuckled.

"Which university did you graduate from?" Leah asked him.

"The University of St. Andrews," he answered. Then he asked, "Which University will you attend?"

"Harvard."

"Congratulations."

"I haven't graduated yet," Leah said to him in all modesty.

"Should I come to your graduation to be sure that you do?" he asked, anxious to see her again.

"I would be quite unhappy if you didn't," she shot back with an assertion that evenly reddened their adorable faces.

"I almost forgot the station porters I brought with me to collect everyone's baggage," he said after catching Rudolf peeking at his wristwatch.

"Our luggage is in Megève," Patrick informed him.

"In that case, my father and I will lead the way straight to the heliport," he replied. Then directed the men outfitted in Wengen Railway Station uniforms to other passengers needing assistance.

"By the way," Maximilian continued as plain-clothed special forces members from the Swiss Army Reconnaissance Detachment 10 discretely followed the group through the train station. "If anyone is wondering how far we are from Lauberhorn, trust me when I say you will arrive in no time."

Soon afterward, Sebastian, Patrick, Leah, and Edith took their seats inside a multipurpose Swiss Air Force helicopter decorated with a red and white neutrality insignia with glaring spiked icicles hanging from the tail end of the aircraft.

"My name is Enzo Schelling," the flight officer told them as he inspected the throttle. "Milo Lagman is your copilot."

While the two pilots, outfitted in identical, green flight suits checked off three more main controls in the cockpit, Enzo continued.

"My aviator callsign is Ringo, and we have almost thirty years of flight experience with the Swiss Air Force between us. On behalf of the Swiss Confederation, I welcome all of you on."

"Yay, Ringo!" they shouted.

As the helicopter traversed over the most glaciated valley in Europe, each passenger excitedly grinned in flight toward Lauberhorn, home to the oldest, longest, and fastest downhill races.

The Lauberhorn ski races

and competitor Fifty-five . . .

Chapter Two
Lauberhorn

*T*hroughout the globe, millions of ski race fans observed the international Lauberhorn ski races via televised broadcast, collectively, with tens of thousands of other spectators on the sidelines. While competitor Fifty-five exhaled a cloud of condensed breath into the cold atmosphere atop snow-capped Lauberhorn, an electronic audible start-tone activated. Then he boldly thrust himself out of a wooden-framed start hut outfitted in a skintight, white, dark-blue, and red ski suit. As he maneuvered his tucked posture and curved ski poles from side to side within the reoccurring snow-white S-turns, the flawless balance of every left and right turn carved coincided with a desire to break his own thirty-year-old, unbeaten record. After he blew through a passageway underneath a railroad overpass known as the Wasserstation tunnel, he glided on a mostly numb right foot. His left knee was weak with pain, and what was left of the feeling in both thighs felt like they were on fire. When a six-digit race clock displayed one minute of race time left, Fifty-five decreased speed as he forced his fatigued body upright and skidded on the edge of his skis into the last two, most challenging, S-turns. Ultimately, a combination of gravity and raw talent contributed to an incredible midair jump and perfect landing on skis before he slid wildly across the finish line into a cushioned safety barrier.

While Nicholas Romanov III—the Russian Federation defense minister—laid in the snow, he listened to the tremendous roar of thousands of devoted followers of all ages, all were waving Russian, tricolor flags. His best friend, who was carrying a six-ounce, sterling silver hip flask filled with beer and vodka, plunged into the snow beside him. Then, as Vice Admiral Gabriel Kolchak, the Russian Federation commander of the Main Military Medical Directorate, wiped his mouth on the sleeve of a coat invented to resist the subarctic weather conditions in Oymyakon, Russia, Nicholas lifted his goggles over his helmet, exposing his green eyes.

"Do you think it was luck?" he asked in Russian.

"Nothing involving the direct descendant of the last Czar of Russia could be that simple," replied Gabriel as he and Nicholas helped each other stand. "Then again, why ask a physician whose opinion doesn't count until a second serving of vodka?"

As Gabriel and Nicholas laughed and took turns sipping from the same flask, eight bodyguards—all armed with 9mm, folding, submachine guns concealed in civilian ski apparel—were approached by Edith and Sebastian.

"I recognize your faces from the forty-fifth Special

Reconnaissance and Special Operations Airborne Spetsnaz Brigade," said Edith. "But I didn't know all of you were transferred to the Federal Protective Service. Congratulations."

"Thank you," said a senior federal law enforcement officer as the Russian security detail surrounding Nicholas and Gabriel stepped aside.

"I'm glad to see you," said Gabriel, smiling.

"I'm glad to be here," Edith happily replied while she and Gabriel gave one another a half-neck bow.

"It's always good to see the world's most famous eastern Slavic cousins," said Sebastian.

"Contrary to what you may think," insisted Gabriel, who grew up troubled by the open secret. "Nicholas and I are not related. That's just a rumor. And nothing more."

When he and Sebastian shook hands, multiple broadcasting platforms live streaming the event had captured the precise moment Nicholas dropped his helmet and goggles to greet Edith.

"Thank you for coming," he told her as they lovingly hugged each other.

"Thank you for inviting me."

"Where is my goddaughter?"

"On the sidelines," Edith answered while they let go of one another.

"Patrick is with her?" he asked, removing the skis from his feet.

"He is."

"Michael?"

"On his way," she told him.

"To Wengen?"

"Megève."

"Megève, it is," he repeated while they waved to his eager supporters. Later, with his skis in one hand and his helmet and goggles in the other, Nicholas, amid thunderous applause, stood triumphantly on the winner's podium.

Twenty-Four hours later . . .

Chapter Three
Megève

*D*o you recommend mulled wine or black coffee?"
Michael inquired in French while standing in a
hallway of ornate, white, marble, stone flooring
and irreplaceable Greek and Italian paintings and
sculptures from the fifteenth and sixteenth centuries.

"I'm a man of simplicity," answered Mr. Basile, the
most renowned, executive chef within the resort commune of Megève.

After Michael and a member of the British Royalty and
Specialist Protection Command were escorted into a private dining room at the Domaine du Mont d'Arbois in the
Auvergne-Rhône-Alpes region of Southeastern France.
Metropolitan Police Officer Pasha Pavlichenko, dressed in
an ivory dinner jacket and black tuxedo pants, sat alone
with his back to the wall at a small, solid-wood table with
rounded edges. At another table nearby, his protectee took
a guess at what Mr. Basile had implied.

"Then you suggest black coffee," said Michael while
mirror-paneled walls reflected the images of five people,
including his own.

"Or hot chocolate," interjected Sebastian as he held up his own cup full of it.

"Hot chocolate sounds like a plan," said Michael, having taken his lifelong friend's word.

"Whipped cream, caramel, or butterscotch?" inquired Mr. Basile.

"Whipped cream," replied Michael.

"Anyone else?" asked Mr. Basile as he looked around.

"Tea," said Leah.

"Right away," said Mr. Basile, bowing his head.

He walked away from a sizable, antique, walnut, dining room table. Then, similarly clothed as Pasha and the rest of the men, Michael returned to sit next to Sebastian and Leah. Gabriel, Nicholas, and Patrick drank Russo-Baltique vodka beside Edith, Leah, and Patrick's wife, Andrea. Despite how much the ladies enjoyed codfish cakes at the same table's other side, they were mindful not to ruin their designer evening dresses.

"Where were we?" asked Michael as candle lights illuminated the spacious room with perfect subtlety. "Running with sandbags, or were we at the part about swimming with bricks at Lake Annecy?"

"Swimming with bricks at Lake Annecy," answered Sebastian as he and Michael chuckled at the recollection.

"What?" asked Leah with a bit of disbelief.

"It's a water survival exercise," Sebastian told his stepsister. "Excluding my mother, who never attended Rosey, Mr. Kessler made everyone at the table swim with a brick."

"My father trained me," said Andrea.

"And you coached me," Sebastian said to his mother.

"You remember that?" Andrea asked him.

"I remember everything you and Patrick taught me as an adolescent and as an adult," replied Sebastian proudly as Andrea and Patrick smiled at each other.

"What does swimming with bricks teach?" Leah asked her stepmother.

"Confidence," Andrea told her.

"Will you show me before I register for Kessler's swim class?"

"Certainly," said Andrea with a smile.

"I wouldn't eat fish cakes anymore if I were you," Gabriel warned Leah.

"They're delicious."

"They're also spicy, and your tea will be hot."

"This is my last one," replied Leah as she, Andrea, and Edith each stuck their forks into one more fish cake.

"Patrick told me when your daughter isn't evaluating US air and missile crew members' health," Andrea mentioned to Edith and Nicholas. "A certain flight surgeon is at home watching the animated adventure film *Mr. Peabody and Sherman*."

"According to Patrick," Edith jokingly shot back. "Catherine could say something similar about the executive director of European Union Aviation Safety and a cartoon called *The Secret of Nimh*."

"When it comes to secrets," Andrea announced to a bunch of giggles at the table. "No one's secret is safe with Patrick. What else did he tell?"

"Dad told me Erich Hartmann is your father," replied Leah, among concern over what the ingenious teen might say. "He also said your father is the most successful fighter pilot in the history of aviation warfare."

"And I miss him very much," said Andrea reacting to her father's revelation with one of her own. "I believe your mother's memory endures through you in the same way the remembrance of my father survives through me."

"Then, you've met my mother?"

"I have not been privileged to meet Kirsten von Oppenheim," answered Andrea. "But your dad told me she was a banker who later became an archeologist like her great-grandfather, Baron Max von Oppenheim."

At that same instant, the executive chef and four waiters, all dressed in black tuxedos, returned to the luxuriant hotel's secluded dining room.

First, a teacup of authentic Chinese Da Hong Pao tea and a vintage, 1950s, Italian-made electric tea kettle were carefully set on the table in front of Leah. Next, a cup of hot chocolate and whipped cream was left for Michael before Mr. Basile and his helpers went away as swiftly as they had appeared.

"Kirsten had always been concerned with preserving ancient relics," Patrick said to no one in particular. "Following our divorce, she partnered with the J. Paul Getty Trust then joined an international team of archaeologists at the Citadel of Aleppo in Syria."

"During the Arab Spring?" asked Michael.

"During its aftermath," answered Leah.

She enjoyed some of the tea before speaking about the most influential person in her life.

"A missile struck the medieval Citadel not long afterward," Leah said. "No one from my mother's team, including my mother, has been seen or heard from since."

"Out of respect for your daughter," said Michael. "I don't want to seem insensitive, but I have to ask about bodies or skeletal remains?"

"Thank you for being mindful of her feelings," replied Patrick. Encouraged by Leah's heartfelt smile. He removed a single Gurkha Royal Courtesan Cigar from a stitched pocket inside his blazer's lining and lit it. After exhaling smoke from the precious Himalayan tobacco leaves packed inside, Patrick continued.

"Regarding the missile attack on Kirsten's last known location, proof of life or death has so far not been confirmed."

"How long has she been missing?" Michael probed.

"Several years," responded Patrick.

"That's not enough to petition for a certificate of a legal presumption of death," said Michael.

"Do you believe my mother is alive?" Leah asked.

Michael took a sip of hot chocolate before he answered her.

"What I know is that two of my cousins were younger than you when they lost their mother," he said. "In other words, I've known pain, but not like that. This is why I empathize with you."

"And I thank you for it," Patrick interjected.

"You and Leah are more than welcome," replied Michael.

"Find Basile," Patrick told Leah. "Tell him we're not to

be disturbed. Then see if other guests on the property require anything."

"But, Dad," Leah replied.

When there was no response, she knew better than to press him further.

"I've enjoyed the camaraderie," Leah said to everyone at the table before closing with Michael. "Please give my warmest greetings to Her Majesty the Queen."

"I will be sure to give her your regards," Michael replied.

Leah kissed her father on his cheek, stood up, and curtseyed.

"It seems like winning the most dangerous ski race for the second time is the furthest thing from your mind," Edith said to Nicholas as Leah walked out.

"I won the Lauberhorn," he emphasized. "The Streif on the Hahnenkamm in the Kitzbühel Alps of Austria is considered the deadliest downhill course."

"Regardless, you look exhausted," admitted Edith. "I know I am."

"The shower and steam rooms in each of the six individual bedrooms of Chalet Alice are immediately available to you and Edith," Andrea informed them as she cut in.

"I leave tonight," revealed Nicholas.

"So do I," Gabriel inserted.

"And so do I," Michael added.

"I'm going with them," Sebastian told Andrea.

"Why?" She asked.

"To join Catherine," answered Sebastian.

"Where is she?"

"In a fascinating region of mountainous terrain north-east of the Arabian Peninsula," said Gabriel.

"Catherine's in Syria?" asked Andrea while Sebastian glanced at Patrick.

"If not already," answered Patrick reluctantly. "She will be."

"To search for Kirsten?"

"To search for individuals indicted by the International Criminal Court," he clarified.

"A hunting party."

"A partnership," Sebastian said to his mother.

"More comparable to siblings than classmates," added Michael.

"At what cost?" demanded Andrea as she looked at her son and Michael. "Your lives, nominations as astronaut candidates, or perhaps both?"

"If necessary," answered Sebastian.

"You're the peacetime commander-in-chief of all uni-fied German Armed Forces," Andrea told Patrick with a pale face and worried eyes. "You can stop Sebastian from going to Syria."

"That decision isn't mine or yours," Patrick told her. "The choice is completely his." While Sebastian thought about how he had not remembered seeing his mother so upset, Andrea made sure her cell phone and keys were in her purse and left when she got up.

"You should say goodbye to your mother and sister," Edith proposed to Sebastian.

"She's right," said Patrick.

"I'll meet you outside," Sebastian told the group, then stood up and wiped his mouth with a white linen cloth.

"I admire their relationship," said Edith as Sebastian headed to where he and Patrick knew Andrea and Leah would be. "Catherine understood Nicholas and I were adamant about her becoming a multilingual speaker, but I've questioned whether or not she believes we love her."

"If I had been able to bond with her," Nicholas wondered aloud in regret. "Maybe she would have chosen to be here with us instead of a country where no place is safe."

"What makes the two of you say such things?" asked Patrick. "Because you fled Madrid for the United States with your wife and unborn child after they endured two assassination attempts?"

"Or because you and Edith traveled to Switzerland and enrolled a then-eight-year-old Catherine into one of the world's most prestigious boarding schools?" Gabriel inserted as he chimed in.

"Because Edith and I abandoned her," Nicholas divulged.

"At Le Rosey, where you two knew she would be safe?" Gabriel fired back. "Confronted with similar circumstances that include would-be assassins still at large, who among us would have done differently?"

In the few soundless seconds it took for Michael to read a text message, Patrick extinguished his cigar's lit end, then continued where Gabriel left off.

"Despite everything," he said, looking at Nicholas and Edith. "Your own sacrifices and the failures of your predecessors were not in vain."

"What do you mean?" asked Edith.

"Many German royalists, including my family and I, support the head of the House of Hohenzollern as constitutional monarch of Germany."

"I, too, am a royalist," Gabriel added. "A lot of other Russians like me are also in favor of a Constitutional Monarchy."

"Even with the heir apparent of the House of Hohenzollern as the legitimate claimant of a restored Russian throne," Nicholas asked.

"Absolutely," replied Gabriel.

"Cecilienhof Palace in Potsdam will go back to your family in the name of Princess Catherine Victoria Romanov of Prussia," Patrick declared to Edith, then to Nicholas.

"Revenue exceeding hundreds of millions in assets from diverse stock and bond holdings once controlled by Nicholas II of Russia shall be recovered by Princess Catherine as well."

"The recovery of priceless hereditary possessions stretches beyond friendship," Nicholas said to Patrick.

"Our connection has nothing to do with this," replied Patrick.

"Then, why?" Edith questioned amid mounting optimism.

"Out of deference,"

"To what?" Nicholas asked.

"A promise my great-grandmother Noémie de Rothschild gave to Russian Empress Maria Feodorovna," Patrick explained to them. "And to Max von Oppenheim on behalf of German Emperor Wilhelm II."

"Restoration of your ancestral titles and property will satisfy terms of the alliance between the houses of Hohenzollern, Romanov, and Rothchild," Gabriel injected.

"Is a line of succession included in their final arrangements?" asked Nicholas.

"Yes," Patrick confirmed. "Your daughter, according to hereditary order, is the heir apparent to the German monarchy."

"Throughout the eleven time zones of the most populous nation in Europe," Gabriel proudly acknowledged. "She is already considered empress of Russia by millions of royalists."

"And if I abdicate as the head of the House of Hohenzollern?"

"Catherine will not only convert unofficially to empress of Germany, queen of Prussia," Michael explained in earnest to Edith. "She will spontaneously inherit one of the greatest fortunes in Europe."

Thirty days later . . .

Chapter Four
Matt-a-Mar Marina

A comfortably dressed young woman sat up on the couch, muted the television in front of her, then picked up a multiband portable radio.

"Echo two . . ." acknowledged the woman as she increased the volume on the mobile receiver.

"Priority one," replied a resident special agent in charge through the radio filter.

"Holding?" she asked.

"Affirmative," he answered.

"Clear . . ." she replied.

Following that, within a hamlet called Mattituck found in the Suffolk County Township of Southold, New York, a middle-aged, US Secret Service protectee was awakened by a series of taps at her door. The assistant to the United States president for the Department of National Security Affairs turned on a light.

"Come in," said Vina with a raspy voice. DJ, a US Secret Service special agent, used fingerprint verification to enter Vina's room, a compact, Belgium-manufactured, bullpup assault rifle slung over her shoulder.

"Is it the dock again?" asked Vina while she and her husband, Martin, rubbed their eyes.

"That dock is nothing more than a money pit," said Martin.

"The marina's fine," DJ told them.

"Then what is it?" inquired Martin. "Another high-level call for your mother?"

"Yes," answered DJ, kissing his and Vina's forehead. "Breakfast will be ready at sunrise. Get some rest, Dad."

"This is supposed to be a family getaway," Martin said as the bedroom door slammed shut, locking behind DJ. "I hope you don't get recalled to Washington."

"This is our weekend," she assured him with a kiss of her own. "At least I was able to temporally get DJ reassigned to protect us."

"This is true," conceded Martin.

After leaving him in bed, Vina—wearing her husband's blue and white pinstriped pajamas—entered their bedroom closet to look for his robe and slippers. She put on a soft robe that coordinated well with a pair of matching slippers that were too big for her feet. Next, she used a separate fingerprint verification lock at the rear of the wardrobe area before stepping into a soundproof office. A photograph of Skeleton Coast National Park taken in flight over the Republic of Namibia, and an oil painting of an eighteenth-century Native American Lenape-Delaware warrior armed with a tomahawk, adorned her cryptic surroundings. Vina sat behind a massive oakwood desk where the desk telephone displayed the time as 05:57 a.m.

As she leaned forward, closer to a miniature sculpture of a bronze cheetah next to the phone's speaker, a steady green light indicating the line was in use replaced the flashing red light. "This is Dr. Greene."

"This General Zahid."

"I can hardly hear you," Vina told him, suddenly experiencing radio frequency interference. "Did they make it to Aleppo?"

"Yes," answered Zahid, almost inaudibly.

"Are they still alive?" Vina asked at the same moment satellite communication was cut off.

Chapter Five
John Fitzgerald Kennedy

*D*uke, a three-month-old Basenji, enjoyed having his fur stroked as United States president, Benjamin Rockefeller held him in his lap. The president was seated closest to National Security Advisor Vina de Costa Greene, Director of National Intelligence James Joyce, and Central Intelligence Agency Director Vincent Bunche in the White House's John F. Kennedy conference room. Secretary of State Christopher Kawānanakoa, Secretary of Defense Paul Gossler, and the Central Command commander, General Sheldon Straight, were seated at the far end of a rectangle-shaped, mahogany, conference room table covered with sporadic water bottles, coffee cups, and folders of confidential information. A few more cabinet members, including Judy Foster, the US ambassador for the United Nations, and US vice president Robert Albion, were also present. Everyone wore business casual attire except Sheldon, who was clothed in a Class Bravo army uniform. Their concentration was divided between copies of the Presidential Daily Brief and televised missile bombardment.

"That strike was caught by one of our reconnaissance

satellites," said James. "Safeguarding our assets against overwhelming aggression is the justification."

"The time-lapse is somewhere in the neighborhood of six hours," said Vincent.

"Which weapons were deployed?" asked Benjamin.

"Synchronized cluster munitions from British Eurofighter Typhoons," said Paul.

"Retaliatory air-to-surface, missile strikes came from Syrian ground attack helicopters," said Sheldon. "They were launched in unison with Syrian hand-held and vehicle-mounted, surface-to-surface missile systems."

"No Russian or Iranian retaliation?" Robert asked.

"None whatsoever," voiced James as additional details were explained further "The entire retaliatory fire mission in Aleppo was directed by a Syrian Arab Armed Forces Special Unit called Qawat al-Nimr."

"Better known as the Tiger Forces," Vincent inserted.

"Support," said Benjamin.

"Support wasn't available to Tiger Forces inside Aleppo," answered James.

"Syrian Army Republican Guards and the Fourth Armored Division were exclusively responsible for the defense of Damascus," Vincent said.

"And the Syrian Marines were involved with security for the port city of Latakia," James claimed.

"Then how were our assets in danger of being overrun in Aleppo?" asked Robert as images of smoldering structures were repeatedly broadcast in the background.

"After they were intercepted at Abdel Mounem Ryad

Street and Al Mutanabbi Street," James clarified. "Opposition, initially estimated at forty to sixty fighters, went above eight hundred."

"With no plausible means of egress," added Sheldon. "Their last transmission was danger close."

"Collateral damage?" inquired Robert.

"Regrettably, Mr. Vice President," Paul admitted. "However, the British have promised compensation."

"Despite Syria having no accusations against the German government regarding civilian casualties before or after they acknowledged supporting British counter-insurgency aircraft," said Christopher. "German Federal Defense Minister Patrick De Rothschild also pledged compensation."

"When the United Kingdom executed the airstrike on behalf of the United Nations," added Benjamin. "Our nation became answerable to consequences, unintentionally or not." He drank a little bit of water, then continued. "Put a rush on appropriate compensation to qualified claimants as stipulated by the Foreign Claims Act."

"Yes, Mr. President," Christopher replied.

"Was Aleppo their last location?" Robert asked.

"No, Mr. Vice President," said James.

He closed his copy of the Presidential Daily Brief, stood up, and stepped over to a colorful interactive 360-degree, 3D, holographic map. As lights were dimmed and coffee was sipped, a holographic information mapping system was rotated to a geographic area between the M45 Syrian highway and the D827 Turkish highway.

"The Bab al-Hawa Border Crossing point is an

international border crossing that separates Syria and Turkey," said James. He steered the mapping system to another holographic image and continued.

"Reconnaissance satellites observed our assets' fleeing Aleppo in a blue, three-door Russian manufactured, Lada Oka hatchback. Roughly sixteen miles to the west of the city of Aleppo is an agricultural town called Atarib. That blue hatchback was later seen traveling on the M45 Syrian highway well beyond Atarib, approximately fourteen miles away from the Bab al-Hawa Border Crossing. The last satellite images captured are of the same hatchback abandoned near the entrance of an underground tunnel we know leads to Reyhanlı."

"What is Reyhanlı?"

"Another rural town off the Mediterranean seacoast in the Hatay Province of Turkey, Mr. President," said Vincent.

"It has become more than evident that these individuals are experts in the acronym I heard a military aid use."

"Survival, Evasion, Resistance, and Escape, Mr. Vice President," Sheldon defined.

"Thank you, General," he replied,

"All except two grew up attending one of Switzerland's oldest boarding schools," said Vina.

"How many are we talking about?" asked Benjamin.

"Six," answered James. "The commander of Germany's largest armed forces battalion is one asset."

"This German commander in question rescinded his nomination as an astronaut candidate with the European Space Agency," said Vina.

"For what?"

"To defend a member of our Special Operations Command," she answered.

"Which is the exact reason a British military commander picked to partake in the same astronaut selection process also withdrew from ESA," Vincent added.

"I understand international cooperation with the apprehension of people accused of inhumane crimes outside the jurisdiction of the International Court," said Robert, bewildered. "But not at the expense of highly skilled, young people forfeiting their opportunity to become astronauts."

"The sentimentalism of the young Canadian Armed Forces commander in chief who took a leave of absence to participate was also puzzling," reasoned Christopher. "But when I learned one of them was born with tentacles that could potentially alter the world, the rationale clarified any misinterpretation of their sacrifices I might have held."

"What rationale?" asked Benjamin while he continued to pet Duke.

"The end of a nuclear threat by a country officially recognized as possessing nuclear weapons according to the nuclear Nonproliferation Treaty," answered Christopher.

"Risk of a Russian nuclear missile attack," Paul added. "Which has been a constant threat since 1949, would no longer be a homeland security concern for the United States Army's One Hundredth Missile Defense Brigade or Forty-Ninth Missile Defense Battalion among other strategic US insurance policies."

"Furthermore," inserted Sheldon. "All remains of American

military personnel buried in Russia during the Russian Civil War will be returned to the United States."

"What is the credibility of this intelligence?" inquired Benjamin.

"The leading source is world-renowned historian Mark Lamont," Christopher told him.

"Lamont is the new British ambassador to the United States," said James as he reached for one of the folders on the table. "I have his file."

"Start with what the British ambassador wants to be reciprocated on behalf of the queen," Benjamin told him as everyone listened intently.

"Political support for a British royal family member favored as constitutional sovereign of an equally restored German and Russian monarchy," Judy presented.

"Lamont discussed the queen's desire for an audience between the proposed monarchy and the Czech Republic, the Slovak Republic, and Poland concerning their roles during the Russian Civil War," recounted Christopher. "This will require an inquiry into the World War I Czechoslovak Legion and the Polish 5th Rifle Division regarding imperial Russian Admiral Alexander Kolchak and seized imperial Russia's gold reserves."

"Lamont also mentioned the queen was optimistic about the United States joining Britain," said Judy. "In what capacity?" asked Robert.

"As third-party facilitation publicly seeking resolution of the matter in advance of a political issue," answered James.

"Hypothetically speaking," said Benjamin as he weighed

the unimaginable. "How would a contemporary German and Russian constitutional monarchy be advantageous to American national security?"

"Nicholas Romanov III is not only the Russian Federation defense minister in command of all Russian armed forces, including Russian nuclear arsenals," answered Paul. "He is the proposed monarch's father."

"Additionally," Vincent added. "Nicholas, head of the Russian imperial bloodline by right of birth, has miraculously earned the loyalty of an overwhelmingly large majority of the Russian military and civilian population in his own right."

"In a nutshell, an American alliance with Nicholas's only child would be invaluable leverage over Russian aggression," said Robert.

"Could be invaluable leverage," explained Vina. "The child that grew up in a boarding school, resentful of her parents, is not only who Queen Elizabeth is endorsing as constitutional sovereign of Germany and Russia. This young woman is one of our assets believed to have entered a tunnel leading to Turkey."

"A tunnel no one has emerged from," deduced Benjamin.

"Precisely," voiced Vina as heads around the table were shaking.

"Without a further indication of life," inserted Christopher as he sat back in his seat and rubbed at the rough stubble he missed while shaving. "Not only is the international task force mission to disrupt state-sponsored terrorism in Syria in jeopardy of failure. Any aspirations of the first post-World War II coalition between Russia and the United States are negated."

"There's still a chance they were caught and brought to Sednaya Military Prison," suggested Vina among growing pessimism that included her own. "Which reminds me of the unassuming fifth asset affiliated with International Tribunals."

"I met him over a year ago at a meeting in Canada," said Judy as she removed her vibrating cellphone from the table and crammed it into her purse. "He's a fascinating man who quickly became the center of attention in the room. If not for the Treaty of Lausanne, more than likely he would be Sultan, and his two children likewise would be prince and princess of a dramatically reduced in size Ottoman nation-state."

"Is his interest in the mission contingent on monarchal restoration?" asked Robert.

"This fifth asset declined to partake in any discussion concerning his hereditary right of birth," Vina told him. "This might not mean anything, but he's one of the two assets not affiliated with the same boarding school."

"Then in exchange for likely losing his life," Benjamin started. "What does he hope to gain?"

"A better life for his children," answered Judy.

"I'm curious to know the names of the would-be Sultan as well as the names of his son and daughter," said Robert.

"The son is Alexander Osman Efendi," Vina answered. "At fifteen, he is the second most senior member of the House of Osman, the ruling family of the extinct Ottoman

Empire. His father is Adad Osman Efendi, and he is the Head of the House of Osman. Adad is also the father of an early-aged, adolescent daughter named Nadia Turhan Efendi. Thus, Nadia is third in the line of the session to the House of Osman."

"Adad is fearful of his children being executed or enslaved inside Sednya Prison if they were to be caught by supporters of Bashar al-Assad," said James.

"Because I want to analyze the appropriate course of action and security considerations needed to create German, Russian, and Ottoman constitutional monarchies," said Benjamin, facing Paul and Christopher. "The secretaries of defense and state have my authorization to undertake a Presidential Study in anticipation of a National Security Directive concerning the proposed monarchies."

"Yes, Mr. President," said Paul and Christopher simultaneously.

"Where were we?"

"Sednaya Prison, Mr. President," James reminded him.

"Where is it?"

"Nineteen miles north of Damascus," Vina told him. "Actionable intelligence concerning recent events inside the prison as well as at a hospital in Damascus came from a senior Air Force Intelligence Directorate officer."

"What do we know about this intelligence officer?" asked Robert.

"While representing Syria at an event in Belarus's capital city, the Air Force Intelligence Directorate officer reached out to the US embassy in Minsk, and defected to the CIA," replied Vincent. "Upon approved diplomatic clearance, General Zahid Ahmadi was discreetly escorted on a three-hour flight to Paris."

"The French internal security agency—DGSI—which was tasked with Zahid's surveillance in France, confirmed when Zahid reached Adad after traveling from Paris to Lyon," James explained. "He provided incriminating evidence of shocking Rome Statute violations at Sednaya Prison and Tishreen Military Hospital. Subsequently, an investigation into crimes against humanity was approved by the International Criminal Court."

"Zahid's actions speak well for themselves, but not his inspiration," said Benjamin as he set Duke on the floor.

"We feel eagerness for the reunification of Syria is behind Zahid's backing of Adad," Vincent said. "Simply put, Zahid's support aligns with his value to Adad."

"At the same time, the People's Protection Unit or YPG, the Free Syrian Army, and the Syrian National Army are evenly opposed to ISIL and the president of Syria," Christopher inserted. "Unfortunately, they're also prone to conflict with each other. Despite that, Zahid—who privately advocates Syria's governance returning to the House of Osman—is respected by a great number of opposition fighters that are willing to die for the House of Osman."

"Out of direction from Zahid, many of these fighters have enthusiastically unified to call themselves Ottoman Defense Forces," added Paul. "These fighters, also known as ODF, are secretly under Zahid's command and control."

"Even though Zahid referenced a high early death rate

inside the prison," Vina injected. "He assured Adad that the Assad government remains convinced of his loyalty, and he can evacuate both of the children out of Syria."

"What else has been alleged by the Syrian intelligence officer?" asked Benjamin, probing further.

After Vina skimmed a quote highlighted in her copy of the Presidential Daily Brief. She closed it, then replied to him hesitantly.

"The maggots that infest the living as well as the decaying remains of prisoners—as claimed by Zahid—are the most thriving form of life inside Sednaya Military Prison."

Ninety-Six hours earlier . . .

"Fair winds are in favor of a northern bald ibis floating in midair, hundreds of miles away from land. Just as the lone migratory seabird glides at low altitude near the surface of the Mediterranean Sea, an aesthetically pleasing, aquatic skyline unfolds above Syrian government territory . . ."

Chapter Six
Latakia Beach

*A*s seawater battered an embankment near a quiet settlement erected along a pristine waterfront in Western Syria, one of the accommodations, a somewhat unattractive ten by ten hut made of pinewood and straw, was occupied by two beautiful people.

"Was that your first rip current?" Tarek, a tall, blonde and blue-eyed man, asked the red-haired woman he was snuggled in bed with.

"Yes," Ariane answered. "What about you?"

"My first also," he admitted. Tarek was enthralled by Ariane's green eyes, which were a distinct family trait. While she gently stroked his face, he said, "But we swam out of it just like Kessler taught us."

"He'd be proud," she said.

"We should tell him," he responded.

"Leah's graduation would be the perfect place," said Ariane. "But I doubt he's coaching. He was already old when you, me, Nina, Gerard, and Michael were still Roseans."

"He might be old, but if he's alive, he's coaching," he replied.

"Then Kessler's one of those people who won't retire?"

"Pretty much," he said.

All at once, a soothing melody filtered into their space, and Tarek sat up to listen.

"You hear it too?"

"And I smell it," replied Tarek as he wrapped one of the bedsheets around his waist like a towel.

He walked closer to the window, pushed aside the curtains, then inhaled the aroma of food in the air. Outside, dozens of people conservatively dressed in common Syrian attire were gathered on Latakia Beach. Squinting their eyes against the smokestacks, women cooked lamb and chicken on the grill. For their part, the men played classical music on wind instruments, while teenaged boys prepared a backgammon board game. It was the youngest, all of whom had rushed into the shallow waves, who saw the military helicopters first. Sixteen of them unexpectedly appeared out of nowhere, flying in a tight, low-level diamond formation.

Everyone on the beach, including the service members onboard the helicopters, waved at one another. As soon as all the aircrafts disappeared from the midday sky, Tarek closed the curtains.

"A group of battle helicopters just flew by," Tarek said while Ariane switched off a lamp. "They looked Russian."

"Because they are," said Ariane as she left the bed to stand directly in front of Tarek. "Aside from Iranian and Syrian warplanes that typically participate in scheduled flight plans, aircrafts within two hundred nautical miles of

Syrian airspace without explicit Syrian government consent are vulnerable to GPS interference, communication
jamming, and long-range missile, defense weaponry."

"We should eat," he urged as she kissed his chest.

"After I penetrate your airspace," she whispered softly.
Then, the two athletically-built high school sweethearts
slowly followed the bedsheet she pulled from his waist to
the floor.

A second to spare . . .

Chapter Seven
Au Revoir . . .

*I*n the hour before the sun's first emergence, a car horn was heard a second time. At that moment, in the thick of anxious stillness, their lips separated.

"It's at least a three-hour drive," said Ariane as she reached underneath her pillow where it lay on a tan cot wide enough for two.

"I know," replied Tarek while examining the wallet she passed him. "Thank you."

"You're welcome."

"Leather?"

"French Moroccan leather," she added while grinning.

"I like it."

"It's yours."

"Where did you get it?"

"From a historic market district in Aleppo."

"Only you could find a high-end French Moroccan leather wallet during a threat assessment," he said with a smile as he looked inside the wallet.

While the car horn blew for the third time, Tarek

stuffed the wallet and several other last-minute things into his luggage.

"Before you go," Ariane said, stopping him in the front doorway of the beach hut. "Know that I'm in love with you, too."

Tarek kissed her nose, then without another second to spare, he stepped away decked out in a dark-grey suit with a white scarf partially draped around his head and shoulders.

Into a Remnant of the Past . . .

Chapter Eight
The Forgotten Cities

A midnight-blue, three-door, Lada Oka hatchback that began its mysterious journey in the shadows of darkness passed a sign that read: "CITY OF IDLIB; 56 kilometers."

"One of our classmates told me to tell you she would see you soon," Tarek, seated in the front passenger seat, told the woman behind him in Arabic.

"I miss her," said Aaliyah, adjusting the black hijab that covered her head and shoulders.

"So do I," replied Tarek as the Oka hatchback crossed off-road into a dry riverbed, unable to sustain residual water without heavy rainfall. "Where are we?"

"Near the forgotten cities of Stylites, Serjilla, and al-Bara," answered Alex, a casually dressed teenage Syrian employed for a one-way drive. "Which also means we're in the area of the seventh-century Arab–Byzantine war that ended with the Islamic Arab subjugation of Roman Syria."

"Your future as a historian and tour guide is assured," Aaliyah told Alex, and everyone laughed.

"We seem to be approaching a valley," said Tarek while Aaliyah drank water.

"As well as another dry riverbed," added Alex.

Then the group turned into the valley before crossing over a different dry riverbed. Later, the second sign that came into view displayed the ultimate destination and distance: "CITY OF ALEPPO; 70 kilometers."

"Something is moving ahead of us," said Alex.

"I see it too," replied Tarek as he discarded empty packets of dehydrated apples and bananas. "It's called more wind, more sand, and a lot more dirt." Everyone giggled until they saw a gathering of dogs devouring the carcass of one of their own in the pack.

"Might be a warning of something worse that hasn't happened yet," Alex said as they passed by the animals. "We have about an hour left. If you're thinking about closing your eyes. Now is the time."

While they drove farther along a string of well-preserved ancient ruins and other endangered human remnants dating back to late antiquity's pre-Islamic provincial period, Tarek and Aaliyah leaned back in their seats, but as the hatchback followed a pathway on Ebla and Apamea's dead cities' edge, no one shut their eyes.

Western End of the Ancient Silk Road . . .

Chapter Nine
Aleppo

A fog of fine, powdery sand swallowed the blue Oka hatchback's exterior as Alex, Aaliyah, and Tarek entered the domain of sprawling hills within the limits of a city estimated to have existed as early as the sixth millennium BC.

"Welcome to the city of Aleppo," announced Alex as the hatchback merged with traffic along a route of partially damaged or destroyed vintage Syrian architecture. A short while later, outside of a densely populated marketplace, established before the founding of the Ottoman dynasty. Alex parked adjacent to posters and banners of Bashar al-Assad, the president of Syria, Vladimir Putin, the president of Russia, and Hassan Nasrallah, the Hezbollah Secretary-General of Lebanon.

"I've never seen anything like this," Aaliyah exclaimed.

"What is this place?" asked Tarek.

"Souq al-Attarine," replied Alex. "The finest place in the world for perfume, cologne, spice, and exotic raw meat."

Tarek studied the photograph of a seventy-year-old male who stood about five feet ten inches, in a full Syrian Arab Armed Forces ceremonial dress uniform.

"I'll bring back some of that cologne Alex bragged about," said Tarek as the hatchback's passenger-side door opened. "It might patch things up with your favorite Frenchman."

"Thank you," replied Aaliyah appreciatively. "But he wants babies, I want marriage, and then there's what Ariane wants."

"Which is?"

"You back in one piece," Aaliyah told him.

They shook hands, then as the vehicle door closed behind him, he wandered toward Souq al-Attarine. The market doors were attached to cast-iron hinges originally smelted during the medieval period. Once they opened, Tarek navigated through a congested alleyway that emptied into a magnificent, cobblestone courtyard with high, vaulted ceilings. At that very instant, he recognized the man standing at an herbs and spices display table—surrounded by three plainly dressed men—as the same person in the photograph on his cellphone. He mentally praised Ariane for planning every move that led him straight to the man he came for.

"You're either exceptionally brave, or you have no idea who I am," the man told Tarek before sniffing cinnamon and nutmeg spices.

"Your name is General Gevargese," Tarek said while splashing a pine forest fragrance sample from a different table on his wrist. "You're the minister of defense for all Syrian Arab Armed Forces. The three men with you are from your elite Fourth Armoured Division."

"Who sent you?" he asked. "The US?"

"The UN."

"What do they want?"

"You."

"For what?"

"Genocide."

"Wait!" shouted Gevargese as Tarek raised a subcompact pistol to eye level.

"Stop moving!" Tarek ordered while the firearms concealed underneath the guards' clothing were now fully exposed.

"Stop moving!" Gevargese quickly echoed to his protectors, who reluctantly froze an arm's length apart from each other. "He has to surrender me to The Hague in the Netherlands."

But then, on impulse, Tarek discharged four rounds, and the market erupted into pure pandemonium. He leaned over the felled bodyguards and defense minister on the ground, then fired four more times. At the same time, a substantial amount of blood pooled out of their lifeless remains. Tarek reloaded while running away from the courtyard, joining everyone else, trying to get out of Souq al-Attarine.

"The eldest child of the Head of the House of Osman has the right to one day claim the throne and become girded with the Sword of Osman . . ."

Chapter Ten
Son of Osman

D o you have sisters?" asked Alex while Aaliyah consolidated a ballistic vest, ammunition drums, and magazines within the compact vehicle's limited space.

"If I get to count my best friend as my sister, then yes," Aaliyah replied as she thought of Ariane.

"I have a younger sister," said Alex with an unfiltered cigarette in between his lips. "Her name is Nadia."

"Nadia is a beautiful name."

"My father named her," Alex told her as silvery-grey smoke sailed out of the window. "He also made plans for Nadia and me to move to Paris,"

"Where is your mother?"

"Dead," he said, teary-eyed. "After my father fled Syria. We were raised by our grandparents, then they died in a chemical attack."

"Who is your guardian?"

"No one," Alex said to Aaliyah, who was kind of surprised. "My sister and I take care of ourselves."

"I'm sorry."

"It doesn't matter," replied Alex while smiling enthusiastically about the future. "We're going to live with our father in France, and everything will be OK."

"I met your father last year," said Aaliyah, reflecting on Alex's charm during a gathering in Canada. "He and one of my childhood friends attended law school together."

"My sister expects to go to law school like our father," said Alex.

"What do you want to do?"

"Graduate from West Point."

"The United States Military Academy?"

"Yes," he responded with a giant smile. "But I don't have high school transcripts, and I'm not a US citizen."

"The odds are against you," said Aaliyah as Alex lost part of his joy. "How bad do you want admission into West Point?"

"More than anything," said Alex passionately.

"Then nothing can stop you," declared Aaliyah, gaining another smile from Alex. "Can I ask something else?"

"Yes."

"What were you supposed to do after driving us to Aleppo?" she asked while unzipping two riffle bags.

"Join General Zahid on the Turkish side of the border."

"Then why are you still with us?"

"I want you and Tarek to come with Nadia and me," he said.

His thoughtfulness nearly left her at a loss for words as she continued.

"How old are you?"

"Almost sixteen," replied Alex very proudly. "But I am a son of Osman, I am a warrior, and I have no fear."

"Everyone's afraid of something."

"What are you afraid of?"

"A promise I made," said Aaliyah thinking of someone close to her heart. "I need a favor."

"Anything!" replied Alex gladly.

"Don't say anything, not even goodbye," Aaliyah told him as she plucked the cigarette out of his mouth. "Just get out, leave the door open, and walk as far away from this vehicle as you can. And most of all, don't look back, not for anything in this world."

While Alex quietly walked out of view, she discarded his cigarette, climbed into the driver seat, and closed the driver-side door. After the rapid assembly and function check of parts for an M249 light machine gun and an M27 infantry automatic rifle that had been stowed in the vehicle's passenger seat next to her, Aaliyah—slipping into a ballistic vest—remembered the last time she saw the face of one debonair Frenchman.

*Wherever you are, and
whatever you do, be in love . . .*

—Rumi

Chapter Eleven
A Debonair Frenchman

Gerard De Gaulle—a native of Ajaccio, a French commune on the west coast of Corsica—stepped onto the terrace of an elegant apartment overlooking Franklin D. Roosevelt Drive and the Williamsburg Bridge from the East River's Manhattan side in New York. The thirty-two-year-old attorney and managing director of the International Monetary Fund seemed uneasy on the last night of summer.

"You look worried," said Nina Maczek, a radiant woman of Dutch and Polish descent.

"Terribly," The brown-haired and brown-eyed Gerard had admitted. He was dressed in a tank top, and shorts and Nina was wrapped in a colorful sundress that paired well with her hazel eyes and sable hair.

"Don't be worried," she told him as they sat on a cozy, outdoor love seat.

"Then don't go,"

"I have important business in France and the Netherlands," she replied.

"You're looking at no better guide."

"I know."

"Yet I'm not invited."

"No."

"Why?"

"Unauthorized disclosure of classified intelligence would be an offense against the United Kingdom and Canada."

"Then why is your face imprinted above a fictitious name in what can only be issued by the Lebanon and Syrian governments?" Gerard asked, as he handed a Lebanese passport and Syrian tourist visa to Nina. "They fell on the laundry room floor when I threw our clothes on top of the dryer. I picked them up and recognized your picture, but clearly not the name underneath it."

"I'm sorry," said Nina.

"For being negligent?"

"For not being honest," she admitted.

"Dishonesty in Syria might be one of the things that keeps you safe," replied Gerard.

"I'm not in Syria."

"You will be," Gerard shot back. "In which case, you'll be involved in one of the deadliest civil wars on Earth."

"Russian military intervention is the counterbalance."

"Nothing has been able to stop the war."

"Per an agreement between Russia, Iran, and Turkey," Nina informed him. "The state of hostilities between the Syrian government and its opposition is strictly forbidden in certain sections identified as safe zones."

"For instance?" he probed with a quirked brow.

"The province of Latakia where Russia operates the Khmeimim Air Base," Nina told him. "Other safe zones are Latakia's port city and a Russian naval shipyard in Tartus's port city. But it's the beaches of Tartus and Latakia that are the main attractions."

"Beaches?"

"Complete with seaside houses and resorts," she answered with a smile.

"In a war zone?"

"A safe zone."

"Am I supposed to feel better?" asked Gerard sarcastically.

"Catherine does."

"She's going with you?"

"I'm going with her."

"That means Sebastian and Michael are going with you?"

"What made you say that?" inquired Nina.

"They're inseparable, or at least they were," answered Gerard. "But there's nothing Sebastian wouldn't do for Catherine or, likewise, I for you."

"Have you forgotten you were also joined at the hip with Sebastian and Michael in Le Rosey?"

"I could never forget the best years of my life spent with my classmates," said Gerard.

"But that doesn't validate traveling to Syria."

Gerard got up to put his elbows on the stainless-steel railing that he leaned on—then continued while gazing at the view of a ferry terminal under construction along the East River waterfront.

"Promise me you'll come back," he urged lovingly.

"I promise," Nina, clinching his waist from behind, gently whispered before she quietly and softly kissed his ear. It did not take long for her and Gerard to fall out of their clothes after that. And then, on the outdoor living space floor, the two high school sweethearts made love beneath a full moon—illuminating the night sky brightly.

Worry does not mean fear,

but readiness for the confrontation . . .

–Bashar al-Assad

Chapter Twelve
Lada Oka

*A*aliya was pulled from her thoughts when Tarek tapped on the hatchback's driver-side window.

"It was Gerard again," Aaliyah admitted to Tarek as he entered through the passenger-side door. "You smell good, by the way. What's the name of your cologne?"

"The cologne is called pine forest, and thanks," he said while throwing on the other ballistic vest. "And as much as he loves you, we both know Gerard would want you alert and safe at all times."

"It won't happen again," she told him, knowing failure to maintain situational awareness could end in needless bloodshed.

"Where's Alex?"

"Hopefully with his sister by now," replied Aaliyah as she merged into traffic on Al Mutanabbi Street. "They should make it to the Turkey border before we do."

"After that?"

"The US embassy in Ankara."

"The German consulate in Istanbul would have been better," Tarek told her. "Assuming they cross the border."

"They'll cross it," said Aaliyah with confidence in her little buddy, Alex. Before anymore was said, all commuter traffic came to a complete stop near Abdel Mounem Ryad Street and Al Mutanabbi Street.

"Contact front!"

"Range?" Tarek requested while staring at the road-block ahead of them.

"Six to eight hundred meters," replied Aaliyah as Tarek pulled out a portable satellite radio.

"Thirteen to Twenty-one," said Tarek into the radio microphone.

"Go ahead, Thirteen," responded Twenty-one through the radio filter.

"Are you clear on the contact front?" Tarek inquired.

"Crystal clear on multiple armored personnel carriers, around a thousand dismounted fighters." Acknowledged Ariane from a black van that had secretly trailed Tarek and Aaliyah from Latakia to Aleppo.

"Is there another way to the Aleppo railway station, Twenty-one?" Tarek probed.

"Negative, Thirteen."

"I wish we were barefoot again," Tarek reminisced over the radio. "Someplace between the sand and the water's edge."

"We will be," Ariane replied at the same time a Russian surveillance aircraft assigned to provide airborne operational support came into sight.

***

"Is it true?" Michael asked Pasha onboard a distinctively glossy, green helicopter.

"Is what true?" asked Pasha as Michael peered through laser, rangefinder binoculars.

"You're the only grandchild of the most lethal female sniper in history?"

"No," replied Pasha. "I have a sister."

"I wonder what she was like?"

"My sister is an Egyptologist."

"I meant your grandmother, Major Lyudmila Pavlichenko."

"She died thirteen years before I was born," answered Pasha. "My mother said she would have been proud of my sister and me."

"Your mother's right," said Michael as he handed his binoculars to him.

"I appreciate that very much," Pasha told him as he watched an overwhelming mass of soldiers enclose vehicular traffic at the intersection beneath them.

* * *

While visual surveillance of the same intersection was conducted from a Russian communications district at Khmeimim Air Base via satellite TV, around 113 miles away from Aleppo, in Latakia, Syria, a Russian Space Force captain read a text message from her phone. "'Defense Minister Sahib Gevargese has been shot and killed,'" said Amorette Samusenko.

"That explains why security police and militiamen became a battalion at the intersection," said Vice Admiral Gabriel Kolchak.

"They're not security police and militiamen," replied Amorette, while commanding military satellite transmissions. "They're members of the elite Syrian 25th Special Mission Forces Division, known as Tiger Force Fighters."

"In one or, possibly, more vehicles somewhere at that intersection," Nicholas started to tell Amorette as he and Gabriel monitored the intersection with her. "One German, one Canadian, one American, and one French citizen—who is also a native of Syria—are with the rebels."

"All we need Tiger Force Fighters to do is execute a safety check at the intersection," injected Gabriel.

"Make sure their battalion commander understands that he's free to do whatever he wants with the rebels," added Nicholas. "But the German, the Canadian, the Frenchmen, and especially the American with them, must be taken into custody—unharmed."

"With all due respect General Romanov," replied Amorette. "That was preplanned with the security police and militiamen. Tiger Force Fighters give no quarter to prisoners or to the wounded. There are no exceptions. Not even for women and children."

"Who is their commander?" asked Nicholas.

"Colonel Xavier Gevargese," she replied.

"Any relation to Defense Minister Sahib Gevargese?" inquired Gabriel.

"The slain defense minister was his father," Amorette responded.

"Raise the Tiger Force commander over the radio," Nicholas told Amorette.

"We've tried multiple times," replied Amorette. "He won't answer."

* * *

"Mishka to Amur," Nicholas said into the receiver of his portable radio.

"Amur," answered Michael via the radio filter from the helicopter hovering in the sky a short distance from the intersection.

"Do you have the Tiger Force commander insight?" asked Nicholas.

"Affirmative Mishka," replied Michael just as Colonel Xavier Gevargese emerged from in between subordinate Tiger Force Fighters.

* * *

"Take aim!" Colonel Xavier Gevargese shouted, and Tiger Force Fighters pointed weapons from offensive standing, kneeling, and prone positions.

* * *

"Put an end to him," Nicholas told Michael at the same instant panic-stricken commuters abandoned their cars at the intersection.

* * *

"I'm pregnant," Aaliyah informed Tarek while people fled the intersection on foot.

"Does Gerard know?" inquired Tarek as he chambered a round into an M249 light machine gun.

"Only you and Ariane," answered Aaliyah while she loaded an M27 infantry automatic rifle.

"As soon as I cover the intersection," said Tarek as he exited the hatchback with the stock of the M249 pressed against his right shoulder. "Make a run for it!"

* * *

"Fire!" Colonel Xavier Gevargese yelled at the same moment that Michael and Pasha squeezed rifle triggers and Tarek returned fire with the fighters that initiated the shooting a split second earlier.

A Tiger Force radio operator and a machine gunner lay on the ground, unconscious with identical torso gunshot wounds inflicted by Pasha, and Colonel Xavier Gevargese lay close by, incapacitated in the same way by Michael.

Ahead of two ODF fighters, Ariane—holding a portable satellite radio—exited the van with Adad.

* * *

"ECHO 29, THIS IS BRAVO 335! IMMEDIATE SUPPRESSION! I SAY AGAIN, IMMEDIATE SUPPRESSION!" Ariane shouted into the radio to a Combined Air Operations center. "GRID 24951302, I AUTHENTICATE QUEBEC, FOXTROT, OVER!"

* * *

"THIS IS ECHO 29, IMMEDIATE SUPPRESSION, GRID

24951302, OUT," responded a Joint Terminal Attack controller assigned to the princess of Phillips's Royal Regiment.

All at once, two Eurofighter Typhoons on airborne alert departed their holding pattern above the Mediterranean Sea. As they navigated toward an arid region of mountainous terrain northeast of the Arabian Peninsula, the British combat aircraft—based out of Akrotiri Royal Air Force station in the Republic of Cyprus—entered sovereign Syrian airspace, with missiles launched at Syrian radar-guided air defense batteries from a German ballistic missile submarine silently submerged underwater about one-half of a mile away from the Port of Latakia.

* * *

"Mishka to Amur," Nicholas said into the microphone of his portable radio.

"Amur," replied Michael, surrounded by the sounds of rapid gunfire Nickolas could hear despite helicopter blades also rotating strongly through his radio filter.

"The Syrian government lost contact with multiple air defense sites," Nicholas told Michael soon after an underwater missile launch had been detected by his district. "Four Syrian Air force interceptors have been defeated by two unidentified aircraft cruising over Syrian territory with impunity. We believe Aleppo has been targeted for an additional release of munitions. Withdraw to Khmeimim Air Base immediately."

* * *

As Aaliyah unleashed ear-piercing, gunfire from behind one of the abandoned cars, Tarek stopped firing, turned around, and ran away from Tiger Force Fighters in a diagonal direction. When everyone saw him fall, he was thirty meters from Ariane, Adad, and ODF fighters, and less than fifteen meters away from Aaliyah.

"Tarek!" both Aaliyah and Ariane shouted.

"I'm OK!" he yelled, although he was visibly in distress.

At the same time, Ariane and ODF fighters continued the exchange of automatic gunfire with Tiger Forces. Aaliyah and Adad made their way through a barrage of bullets to Tarek.

"Can you walk?" Aaliyah asked Tarek as Adad provided rear security.

"I can try," he told her.

While Aaliyah pulled off her belt and tied it above two bullet holes in Tarek's bloodied left leg, Adad shot and killed a Tiger Force Fighter aiming a rocket-propelled grenade launcher in their direction.

"Stand up!" Aaliyah hollered at Tarek.

At the very moment they pulled each other up, Aaliyah and Tarek collapsed underneath the weight of Adad, who had fallen backward on top of both of them. All the while, Tarek, yelling in pain, gripped his bleeding leg. Aaliyah desperately tried to stop more blood loss from a massive hole in Adad's neck as Ariane, and the two ODF fighters dived to the ground near them. Then, when ODF fighters took over the exchange of gunfire, Ariane checked Adad's airway. "He's not breathing," Ariane cried out. A moment later, she said, "He's dead."

"Put your arms around our shoulders, classmate!" Aaliyah told Tarek amid bullets slamming into the dirt.

"Once we lift each other, we have to run!" added Ariane.

"Then on one, two, three . . ." yelled Tarek.

When he put his arms around Ariane and Aaliyah, ODF soldiers raised Adad's body. But, as soon as they stood up, a hypersonic munition detonated. The blast wave created superheated-blast winds that laid waste to multiple motor vehicles and occupied buildings nearby.

* * *

In the explosion's aftermath, sweltering heat rose from cars and structures lit ablaze, dark plumes of smoke reduced visibility, and warm blood ran from the dead and living alike.

"Don't use your hands," Aaliyah warned Ariane. "Metal takes longer to cool than flesh."

Ariane pushed burnt pieces of rubble off her legs with the barrel of a weapon that landed within arm's reach of her. After that—by a miracle—she was able to slide in the sand toward Aaliyah.

"No!" yelled Aaliyah, sensing she might be bleeding to death as blood flowed from her nose, mouth, and ears.

"Can you crawl out of there?" Ariane asked, noticing Aaliyah appeared trapped in debris beside both ODF combatants killed by the bomb.

"A big piece of metal is sticking out of my hip," she

replied, wheezing in intervals between inhaling super-heated fumes packed with fine particles floating in the air. "Save yourself and Tarek."

Once Ariane crawled to him, she found Tarek covered in a mixture of sand, ashes, and a lot of blood that mainly was Adad's. She placed her ear above his mouth and began to look, listen, and feel.

"He's breathing!" Ariane shouted.

Then Aaliyah motioned for Ariane to look at the blue Oka hatchback deserted at the beginning of the battle. Realizing it had, incredibly, only sustained moderate damage and the engine was still running, Ariane eagerly untangled Tarek from the wreckage he was also partially twisted in.

"The only way out now is by tunnel," said Aaliyah, pausing to cough as Ariane dragged Tarek to the hatchback and loaded him into it.

"I can't leave my navigator," Ariane cried, and the sounds of voices from an increasing number of Tiger Force Fighters could be heard around the destruction of collapsing buildings and car alarms.

"You're the navigator now," Aaliyah shot back in between severely labored breaths.

"But—"

"Take the car, the German, and go!" interrupted Aaliyah as the tremor of the infantry boots and voices of Tiger Force Fighters became dramatically more pronounced. "This is the last order I give you."

At the same time Aaliyah gasped her final breath, two

British Eurofighter Typhoons released precision-guided missiles in the direction of Aleppo. As a result, numerous Tiger Force Fighters in control of the vicinity were, unknowingly, in jeopardy of obliteration. By now, unconscious, battered, and bloodied, Tarek was left spread out across part of the front and rear seats. And Ariane—sobbing inconsolably with superficial injuries on her head, face, and chest—drove the blue Lada Oka hatchback straight into a bright haze of red-hot embers and curls of dense black and grey soot.

Banff National Park, Alberta Canada

One Year Earlier . . .

Chapter Thirteen
Lake Louise

As a rabbit foraged for food near the shoreline of an ancient glacial lake named after a nineteenth-century British princess, a shiny red canoe—mostly made of northern white cedar wood—slowly but steadily propelled forward.

"There is nothing like the warmness of the sun on a crisp early morning," said Edith in German-accented English, paddling through a mist of fog widely scattered over a tranquil body of water, with her daughter. "That's what Grandfather Louis Ferdinand use to say on days like this."

"Did Grandfather ever—" Catherine started before the abrupt appearance of an Osprey in a ninety-degree accelerated dive.

"Did he ever what?" asked Edith while the bird of prey carried a fish away from the lake.

"Did he ever discuss his brother?"

"Following my father's death, his focus was preparing me for an impending restoration of the monarchy. He preferred word choices like 'impending,' 'inevitable,' and 'eventually' upon any utterance of restoration. Nevertheless," she remarked, pausing to loosen a scarf covering her neck and shoulders. "I remember talk of a connection between Hitler and every prince of the fatherland."

"What sort of connection?" asked Catherine.

"Closely-guarded jealously."

"I don't understand."

"Nazi Germany was grief-stricken after Uncle Wilhelm died in combat during France's invasion," explained Edith. "Crowds drawn to his funeral unexpectedly rose to a historical level. Hitler couldn't risk the Nazi Party's imagine or his own, being dominated in public again—least of all by a second German prince's battlefield death."

"What did Hitler do?" asked Catherine.

"He outlawed royal princes from serving in the German armed forces, but not in the Nazi Party."

"Grandfather entered the Nazi Party?"

"He joined the resistance against it," answered Edith.

At that moment, except for the sound of oaring, quietness engulfed the canoe as the surface of the lake's distinctive greenish-blue waters spread out into full view beneath strong sunshine and dense fog. Then in the wake of a short period of nostalgia, Edith continued.

"After Grandmother Kira's passing, I was granted the title 'Grand Duchess of Russia,' and Grandfather Louis began speaking about my future as 'Guardian of the Throne.'"

"Are there any of his lectures that you remember most of all?"

"Certainly," replied Edith. "One, in particular, was

concerned with the necessity of handling affairs with equal fluency in the Russian, German, French, and English languages."

"Is that why you left me at Le Rosey, crying for my mother, when I was eight?" asked Catherine resentfully.

"Part of it," answered Edith.

"And the other part?"

"Immeasurable sacrifice and compassion," replied Edith remorsefully.

By the time the red canoe had approached a wooden dock outside the Lake Louise Fairmont Chateau, the tension between mother and daughter that lingered was invisible. Their morning meal consisted of olive wagyu-beef steaks grilled until they were medium rare and juicy. The French toast, made from scratch, included maple syrup from the world's only maple syrup reserve out of Laurierville, Quebec. Drinking glasses held water sourced from freshwater icebergs broken off from Greenland's glaciers. Last but not least, a few ounces of Black Beluga caviar coated scrambled egg whites. When they finished eating, Edith and Catherine rode away from the 539-room, five-star resort in a black limousine driven by a Royal Canadian Mounted Police officer dressed in plain clothes. The pennant of the governor general of Canada, displaying a crowned lion carrying a red maple leaf on a wreath of red and white colors across a blue backdrop, was attached to the front end of the Canadian government vehicle.

Chapter Fourteen
Three Sisters

*A*bout one hour away from Lake Louise at the far end of Canmore's town, in Alberta, Canada, stood an impressive 8,010-square-foot, three-level place of residence. The estate was almost entirely hidden by dense forest near the Three Sisters mountains. The six-bath and six-bedroom, timber-framed property Edith inherited twenty years earlier served primarily as the ideal private getaway.

"When was this taken?" asked Donnie Nowak, as he admired a well-preserved photograph of nine European kings.

"Circa 1910," answered Edith, seated next to Catherine and Donnie on an oversized, black, U-shaped leather couch. "Four years before the presumption that World War I would end all wars."

When Edith rose from the couch that also accommodated officials representing Canada, the United Kingdom, the United States, France, and the International Criminal Court, Donnie returned the framed picture.

"But forgive me," Edith continued as she walked

around a well-polished, nickel-plated coffee table made to look exactly like a tree stump. "I nearly forgot why we're here."

"A picnic," Donnie reminded her with a polite smile and a neatly folded letter in hand.

"That was the announcement on your invitation," Nina Maczek responded as Edith hung the picture on the wall of a lavish room featuring lofty ceilings and a grand stone fireplace. "But that's not why you're here."

"Then may I ask why, Your Excellency?" requested Donnie while discarding the letter.

"According to the Letters of Patent, signed by His Majesty King George VI," explained Nina. "The highest-ranking Canadian Supreme Court Justice is equally a deputy of the governor general of Canada."

"Ten other adjudicators can serve as a deputy of the governor general," Donnie fired back while Edith sat beside her daughter.

"Only you as chief justice or Britta Warburg as senior puisne justice can function as administrator of Canada," replied Nina.

"Neither Britta—who is currently in Israel for her nephew's bar mitzvah—nor I can act in that role unless . . ."

"I'm dismissed, incapacitated, or absent," said Nina, interrupting Donnie.

"An absence is the only thing I would remotely predict," Donnie told Nina, guessing out loud.

"A six-month absence," Nina confirmed. "Which is

why on the Prime Minister's guidance and at the pleasure of Her Majesty the Queen, upon your acceptance, I give you full autonomy over my Regimental Horse Guards and Grenadier Guards as well as control over my most senior infantry regiment, my beloved Foot Guards."

"When do you need my answer?"

"Now."

"In that case, I accept."

"Then effective immediately, on behalf of her Majesty the Queen," Nina told him as everyone stood. "I, at this moment, appoint you, Donnie Nowak the Honorable, the deputy of Her Excellency to take over all powers and responsibilities as the commander in chief and governor general of Canada."

"Congratulations," Thomas Arthur, secretary to the governor general, said to Donnie with a smile.

As extra praise and well-wishing followed, others present on the retreat's main level, such as an American bureaucrat next to her security detail of Special Agents with the United States Diplomatic Security Service and a French administrator with uniformed Royal Canadian Mounted Police officers, rendered compliments as well.

"A small ceremony concerning the temporary transfer of power will take place tomorrow at Rideau Hall," said Thomas after Donnie thanked everyone.

"Why? Are you leaving us, if you don't mind me asking?" probed Donnie, gambling Nina might say more than she already had.

"I have to take care of unfinished business inherited

from my great-great-grandfather," replied Nina. "Have a safe trip, and I'll see you in six months," responded Donnie as he stood up to smile and shake hands with one of the most evasive women he'd ever known.

"Six months," replied Nina with a grin that lasted all the way to a massive entryway.

Afterward, two Royal Canadian Mounted Police officers accompanied Donnie and Thomas outside before they crossed through the estate's front gate in a black, extended-length, sports utility vehicle.

* * *

"In my role as investigatory powers commissioner for the United Kingdom," Edith started. "No other point in time has been more uncertain. That is why not only am I pleased to announce that Nina has graciously accepted a temporary appointment as an inspector with my office, but I'm equally delighted that a spokesperson from the International Criminal Court, as well as an ambassador to the UN, has joined us."

After a bit of impromptu handclapping, Edith continued.

"I think introductions related to the threat reduction objectives our ICC partner will expand on later are in order, starting with a recent Pulitzer Prize-winning writer."

"Thank you, Commissioner Prussia, for the warm welcome," said the ambassador to Edith with a bright smile. "As most, if not all, in the room know, my name is Judy Foster, and I'm the US ambassador for the United Nations. On behalf of President Benjamin Rockefeller, the United States is firmly committed to assisting the international community with security. In that regard, I kindly yield the floor to our esteemed colleagues preparing for direct action."

"My name is Nina Maczek," Nina said. "Nuclear power instructor for the Canadian Joint Incident Response Unit was the position I held before my appointment to governor general."

"My name is Catherine Romanov-Prussia, and I'm currently a flight surgeon with US Air Force Special Operations Command," said Catherine. "I was a Nuclear power operator for the US Defense Threat Reduction Agency prior to attending the Temerty Faculty of Medicine, which is the University of Toronto's medical school."

"Proceeding on the same track," said the court official. "On behalf of Chief ICC Prosecutor Fatou Matupi, thank you, Commissioner Prussia, for hosting this event. Perhaps not everyone knows that the International Criminal Court's office of the prosecutor is made up of the Investigation, Prosecution, Jurisdiction, Complementarity, and Cooperation Divisions. I am the deputy prosecutor in charge of the Investigation Division, and my name is Adad Osman Efendi. I became a recipient of the Legion of Honor during my first tour in Afghanistan with the French Foreign Legion's 2nd Parachute Regiment. Afterward, I received French citizenship, then admittance into Paris 1 and Sorbonne Law School."

"Which is where you met Gerard," said Nina smiling.

"What else did Gerard say?" he asked with a grin.

"You're the reason he graduated Sorbonne."

"He's the reason I graduated," Adad shot back as he chuckled, the laughter was contagious, and the rest of the room joined. "Now he's a banker, and I, in a roundabout way, turned policeman."

After a few more laughs and sips from water bottles, an aid passed to everyone, Adad returned to his seat and continued.

"While examining the evidence for and against two individuals equally presumed innocent, I gathered enough proof for the ICC to indict one of them for war crimes."

Judy removed a laptop stored in an old, leather bag she carried everywhere, and the room remained readily patient. When she set the government-issued computer on top of the shining coffee table, Edith made a gesture that meant it was OK for her to proceed. Then everyone observed a picture of an Asian woman on the computer screen wearing a Soviet-era-inspired North Korean naval officer's peaked cap and captain's rank on a black jacket covering a blue shirt.

"Kimberly Wang is a middle-aged heterosexual who many men have described as very pleasing to look at," Judy, pointing at the picture, said as she explained further. "This senior captain who serves in the Korean People's Navy holds a doctor of philosophy in nuclear engineering from the Massachusetts Institute of Technology. Her expertise is magnetic fusion technology and plasma physics. She is unmarried and doesn't have any children, as far as we know. In addition to illegally acquiring advanced uranium enrichment technology, Kimberly manufactured and distributed Improvised Explosive Devices."

"These IEDs have been used to slaughter combatants and noncombatants alike in Iraq, Afghanistan, and Syria," Adad inserted. "Because the ICC has limited jurisdiction in Iraq and none in Syria, Kimberly can only be seized for the tribunal at The Hague in the Netherlands for war crimes in Afghanistan."

Judy opened a second picture on the laptop of a man seated in the captain's chair of an all-purpose, aluminum fishing boat. While the photograph of the man wearing a multicolored, cotton-head covering and a long, one-piece, black, linen kaftan was studied, Adad continued.

"His name is General Sahib Gevargese," he revealed. "He's the minister of defense for all Syrian Arab Armed Forces. He is also responsible for ordering the extermination of every prisoner of war he's captured as well as their families. His crimes are comparable to genocide, an Article 6 violation of the Rome Statute."

"Is Sahib solely in violation of Article 6?" Catherine inquired, as her mother faced Adad.

"No," he acknowledged. "His son Xavier Gevargese is the main accomplice, but Sahib is your best ticket for at least one of two things, or both."

"Which are?" asked Nina.

"Admittance into Tishreen Military Hospital or, upon capture, execution," answered Judy as she pointed to a picture of the hospital on her computer. "According to New Zealand, Britain, Canada, the United States, and Australia, Kimberly oversees a Syrian weapons program manufacturing internationally banned chemical weapons at an underground Tishreen Military Hospital facility. To be clear, Tishreen Military Hospital in Damascus should not be confused with Tishreen University Hospital in Latakia, which was my mistake. Having said that, we believe the best chance, or even the only chance, to apprehend Kimberly will be at Tishreen Military Hospital."

"While my son, Alexander, transports Nina and Sebastian from Latakia Beach to Aleppo," said Adad, and Catherine and Nina glanced at each other. "In another vehicle, about an hour behind them will be me, Catherine, and two fighters from the newly created Ottoman Defense Forces. Once Alex, Nina, and Sebastian drive into Aleppo, Nina will take over the vehicle, and my daughter, Nadia, will be waiting for her big brother Alex at a safe house. Both children know the way to a tunnel underneath the border between Syria and Turkey. Alex has until one hour after nightfall to reach his sister before they start for the tunnel together, or she leaves alone. Then, assuming all goes well, the American embassy in Ankara is where my children will wait for us."

"Risk," said Catherine.

"Significant," Edith affirmed while Adad removed two passports and tourist visas from his leather bag.

"It's imperative to forget everything you remember about your true identity," Adad told Catherine and Nina.

He handed a Lebanese passport and a Syrian tourist visa to Nina. Then gave Catherine a separate Syrian tourist visa and Russian passport.

"May I?" Adad asked Judy while reaching for her laptop.

"Certainly," she replied to the request.

"What's your name?" Catherine asked Nina as Adad clicked on a downloadable computer file.

"Aaliyah Akkari from Lebanon," answered Nina.

"My name is Ariane Dmitriev of French and Russian descent," Catherine told her as Adad finished downloading a digital folder.

"General Sahib is known to shop with at least one bodyguard in a marketplace called Souq al-Altereen," he said

"Where is Souq al-Altereen?" Nina asked.

"In the city of Aleppo," answered Adad as he pointed to the computer's map. "It is within the alleyways of this ancient Souq that you will find the general."

"And when we find him?" prompted Catherine.

"Someone appointed to protect you will assassinate Sahib," Edith told Catherine.

Adad uploaded a German military officer's image wearing a gray uniform and green beret.

"His name is—"

"Sebastian," Catherine interrupted, recognizing the man she had known since they were both children.

"I understand you attended school with him."

"We both did," Nina said to Adad.

While she swallowed a mouthful of water, Adad continued.

"En route to the Aleppo railway station where Sebastian Hartmann will only be known as Tarek Nazari," he said while powering down the laptop. "Your position is expected to be intercepted. That is also where all of us will fight side-by-side. Ultimately anyone suspected of being involved with Sahib's killing will be brought to Sednaya Prison alive. Within this prison, also known as the Garden of Elephant Chains, a sixth asset will arrange our release, cross-border escape, and reunion with my children."

"But if you make it," declared Edith. "If you withstand armed conflict against Syria's most elite fighting force, it will only mean the beginning."

"The beginning of what?" asked Catherine.

"Indefinable suffering," replied Edith amid a tearful farewell.

Seventeen Miles North
of Damascus, Syria Sednaya Prison . . .

Chapter Fifteen
Garden of Elephant Chains

*A*s the Syrian Air Force Intelligence director entered a degraded prison auditorium, a gold insignia indicating the rank of a general adorned his desert camouflage uniform. Military police officers, all dressed alike in camouflaged woodland uniforms, stood beside, behind, and in front of each other. With boot heels placed together and feet positioned at a forty-five-degree angle. Each man in the military formation stood with their chest out, chin up, and hands aligned along the seams of trousers. But the young Air Force Intelligence chief felt nauseated. So, he removed a small, hand-sized plastic bottle from his hip pocket and opened it before addressing Captain Mahdi Hamanti. "Have your men fall out," General Zahid Ahmadi told him.

"Fall out and carry on!" Mahdi loudly instructed a subordinate officer after briefly turning away from Zahid, who had already begun dabbing what remained of peppermint oil underneath his nostrils.

"I assumed death was second nature to the general," said Mahdi as thirty-two, compulsory enlisted men returned to assigned duties.

"Not the smell of it," replied Zahid.

Once he discarded the empty bottle, the inspections started. Zahid noticed the central nervous system of one of the prisoners appeared catastrophically impacted by shock.

"How many males have been electrocuted?" Zahid questioned Mahdi.

"At least two hundred," answered Mahdi. "But preventing permanent injury to the healthiest selected as replacements for our labor force has become more of a challenge."

"Why?"

"Doctor Kimberly Chang, our top North Korean military advisor, doesn't need consent to transfer Sednaya prisoners to Tisheren Hospital." Mahdi vented.

"For medical treatment?"

"Medical attention is a rare opportunity," He disclosed to Zahid. "Most, if not all, of the transfers she orders are concerned with experimentation and analysis."

"Of what?"

"Human exposure to biological, chemical, and radioactive weapons."

"Xavier knew better than to approve prisoner reassignment ahead of an Air Force Intelligence interrogator," said Zahid outraged.

"I beg your pardon, General," said Mahdi. "The prison commander never gave authorization."

"Who did?"

"President Assad," answered Mahdi, and Zahid was forced to concede to the fact that the well-being of the individuals he had come for was unclear.

"Where are the rebels?"

"Behind us," Mahdi said, and they turned around.

"Were they breathing when they got here?" Zahid inquired, staring at about a dozen bodies stacked against a wall.

"Ten of them were," replied Mahdi, then pointing to Nina and Adad. "But those two were killed in battle against the twenty-fifth Special Mission Forces Division, which is the same battle that, as you know, took Xavier's life."

"What happened before Xavier left?" asked Zahid.

"He became hysterical after notification of his fathers' assassination," Mahdi explained. "Xavier only butchered one of the men before leaving. I summarily executed nine others after that."

"By Xavier's direct order?"

"By mine," said the voice of a man much older than Mahdi and Zahid.

Then Lieutenant Colonel Salah El Sayed, a man known for unnecessary violence, especially against women and children, appeared.

"Unless a man knew better," Salah continued while patting eucalyptus oil below his nostrils. "He might think the Air Force Intelligence Service intends to prosecute him over dead government rebels, or more specifically, the death of Prince Adad and his son."

"Per the Treaty of Lausanne signed before any of us were thought of including you," Zahid informed Salah. "Adad was not a prince, and neither was his son if indeed he is dead."

"And if he is?"

"At the same time, any execution before Air Force interrogations is an illegal killing," Zahid told him. "I believe your allegiance to Syria should be celebrated, not prosecuted."

"That was generous of you," said Salah as he and Zahid exchanged a deceptive stare. "Please follow me."

In the same direction of echoing screams for help from captives deprived of food, medical assistance, and sanitary conditions, Zahid was directed past a honeycomb of dilapidated holding cells and other neglected spaces needing major masonry repair work. Eventually, the executive prison commander led the way into a room where a teenager swung shoulder to shoulder with another man by the same rope hooked to the ceiling.

"This is Adad's son," said Salah. "He and the German national next to him were found in a tunnel with an American."

Zahid was secretly more than glad to see Alex alive despite the traumatic injuries that riddled the youngster's body.

"My name is General Zahid Amandi," he told the German. "As commander of Air Force Intelligence, I have the power to set you lose. But—I promise you, if you lie to me, I will send you to the prison crematorium and personally watch your cremation—while you're still alive."

Zahid took a moment to compare their injuries, then continued as Tarek—barely conscious—listened.

"I'm going to ask you one time and one time only," he said. "If your name is Sebastian Hartmann, and you illegally entered Syria to fight against the Syrian government, please nod your head. If that's not true, shake it."

Despite the agonizing pain, Sebastian—a bloody mess of man—nodded his head, yes.

"My interrogators are waiting outside to take him and the boy, as well as the body of the boy's father and the deceased Canadian female, to our Damascus headquarters," Zahid told Salah.

"Cut them down," Salah ordered Madhi.

As soon as ropes suspending them in the air by their arms were clipped, Alex and Sebastian hit the dirt floor hard. After Madhi put an eleven-inch spear pointed bayonet back into an olive-colored sheathe hidden inside his left sleeve, he began detaching their chains.

"Now I want the American," said Zahid.

"I don't have her."

"Where is she?"

"Tisheren Hospital," replied Salah as Zahid nodded in gratitude.

"By the way," said Zahid. "I understand we're both looking for Adad's daughter. If you happen to find her before me, I don't want her harmed."

"She won't be," replied Salah, who now wanted the source of who leaked his intentions as much as he craved the daughter Adad left behind.

When Zahid walked toward the same passageway he emerged from, he had no doubt Salah would kill Nadia unless he found her first.

One of the Oldest Cities on Earth . . .

Chapter Sixteen
Jasmine

While Pasha stood with Russian Federal Protective Service members, screening access points to an eight-foot-wide hallway at Tishreen Military Hospital, Nicholas and Michael leaned against a wall near a photograph of Syrian President Bashar al-Assad, in the same hallway.

"Sebastian is severely wounded," said Nicholas, reading off a text message.

"And Nina?" inquired Michael as Nicholas stood away from the wall to answer.

"She didn't make it," he said, stirring emotions.

"We grew up together," said Michael pacing the hallway with watery eyes. "I should have been there."

"You were there."

"In a helicopter!"

"Protecting them from being overrun!" Nicholas loudly fired back. "I'm sorry about Nina, but you and Pasha are the only reasons I'm making two death notifications instead of four. There was no way Catherine and Sebastian would have made it otherwise."

He didn't have to admit it; it was in his eyes. His older cousin was right, and he appreciated it as he stopped walking back and forth.

"I knew the loyalty of a Syrian government general that defected to the United States was with an Ottoman prince," said Michael, changing the subject. "But I didn't know that same general defected to Russia before defecting to the U.S.,"

"I commend the agents who obtained that secret information for your government," replied Nicholas, praising the agency he understood was none other than the Secret Intelligence Service MI6. "Zahid wanted Adad's children as well as his body, and we wanted Sebastian and Nina. His job was to provide your fellow assets with safe passage out of Sednaya Prison, and he did. Now Adad's daughter's life is in jeopardy, and Zahid is desperate to rescue her. So, I said that his convoy will be allowed to travel to Turkey safely before turning around to save an ancient ancestral tomb despite my redeployment orders."

"To where?"

"Ukraine," replied Nicholas as the door of the examination room opened in front of them. "General Romanov," a Russian female nurse said to Nicholas.

"Yes."

"Doctors Kolchak and Chang have asked for you," she said, and Nicholas hurriedly passed by her, leaving Michael in the hall.

"Hello, Nicholas," Kimberly, dressed in a white coat

that covered sky-blue scrubs, softly uttered, with Gabriel, also outfitted in scrubs, smiling in the background.

"Hello," he whispered, approaching closer. "It's been a long time."

"A very long time," replied Kimberly as they stood over a young woman lying in an electronic hospital bed.

"Is she my daughter?" asked Nicholas.

"According to DNA paternity testing," answered Kimberly as Gabriel left to give Michael the same news in the hallway. "You cannot be eliminated as her biological father."

"Then she—" said Nicholas before he cut himself off, choked with overwhelming gladness.

"Yes," Kimberly affirmed, then proceeded with the patient's medical condition. "I'm concerned about her brain and breast."

"What's wrong with her?" asked Nicholas.

"She was involved in an explosion that not only left her right breast bruised and swollen," Kimberly explained as the patient gradually opened her eyes. "The blast also gave her a concussion."

"May I speak with her?" Nicholas requested while his daughter stared at him.

"Please don't excite her," said Kimberly as she looked at a pale and disorientated woman with a blood-stained bandage covering her head.

"Where am I?" she asked.

"Tishreen Military Hospital in Damascus," answered Nicholas with a friendly smile. "Also known as the city of Jasmine."

"How did I get here?"

"Hezbollah," he replied.

"I was arrested?"

"Rescued," Nicholas clarified. "Despite the inadequate air quality, Hezbollah fighters were the first to reach you in a crude underground tunnel."

"Is that where I lost consciousness?"

"We think so," he replied as she looked around her hospital room in despair.

"I should be dead."

"So should the German," said Kimberly, chiming in.

"Tarek survived?" she asked with a glare of optimism in both eyes.

"If you're referring to Sebastian," Kimberly informed her. "The answer is yes."

"How did you know his name?"

"I know both of your names."

"But I don't know yours," she replied, while an eighteen-gauge needle was being prepared.

"You should," Kimberly told her as she administered a sedative into Nicholas's daughter's intravenous line.

"Why should I?" she asked.

Once the needle had been discarded, Kimberly began peeling away at the synthetic facial layers concealing her natural face.

"My name is Kirsten von Oppenheim," said Kirsten as her voice transitioned from an adopted North Korean accent to a German dialect. "I'm your godmother."

"My God," said the patient after most of Doctor Kimberly

Chang's false facial impression had been removed. "I've found you."

"As I've likewise found you, Catherine," Kirsten replied.

"My name is Ariane."

"Your name is Catherine Victoria Romanov of Prussia," interrupted Nicholas. "And in 1991, you were born on board a Dutch cargo ship anchored off the coast of the United States Virgin Islands."

"How did a Hezbollah fighter come by that information?" asked Catherine, tiredly.

"I'm not Hezbollah."

"Then, what are you?"

"Your father," answered Nicholas just before Catherine closed both eyes.

At the exact moment he kneeled beside the bed—praying for her recovery—Catherine felt like she was floating in crystal-clear water as she drifted off into a deep sleep.

Forty-Eight Hours Earlier . . .

Chapter Seventeen -
Orange and Red Shades

As Catherine floated on her back, her face was partially submerged at cheek level with the warm and glistening, blue Mediterranean Sea's surface.

"Ready?" Sebastian asked as he held her steady.

"Yes."

"Then you're on your own," he told her as he removed his hands from underneath her shoulders and off her buttocks.

"Come with me," she said while he evenly aligned his body in the water on the opposite side of hers.

"Where?"

"Four Corners Monument," she answered, her eyes still closed. "The only place where the US state borders of Arizona, Colorado, New Mexico, and Utah touch."

Not long afterward, east of a cloudless oasis of warmth and serenity, came two, low-flying, Russian fighter jets moving through dry air at supersonic speed. Within a matter of seconds, Catherine and Sebastian had been swept away from Latakia Beach by high-energy, shock waves rising behind twin warplanes piloted four times faster than the speed of sound.

"We're caught in a rip current," Sebastian shouted, floating twenty-five feet beyond Catherine.

"I feel like I might go under," Catherine called out frantically, while attempting to swim against powerful ocean currents.

"Do you remember what Kessler said?" asked Sebastian before he took a breath.

"Focus on exhaling," she asserted as they were dragged farther out to sea. "Inhale every five strokes."

"We have to swim abreast of the beach," Sebastian told Catherine while she sucked in some air. "You're closer to it than I am. I'll follow you."

A short while after that, they swam out of the rip current and into mild ocean waves that ultimately led to a sandbank, where they collapsed. As they regained their breath, they saw a reptile of some kind crawl along the sand.

"What do you think it is?" he asked as the small four-legged vertebrate crept closer to the same waves that swashed and rippled around them.

"A green sea turtle."

"It's black."

"It's supposed to be," Catherine said as she picked it up. "It's a hatchling. The black coat is camouflage."

She released it and continued.

"Something must have disturbed it. Sea turtle hatchlings are not known to appear on a beach until after nightfall under the cover of darkness. That is how the species instinctively avoids carnivorous animals capable of surprise attacks by air or land in advance of threats from predatory marine life at sea."

"Sounds like a textbook definition of no chance," he said by the time the hatchling reached the water. "I never would have guessed our high-stake gamble was on par with the destiny of a turtle hatchling."

"When you put it like that," she said thoughtfully, as the hatchling vanishes into the depths of the Mediterranean. "It leaves me wondering—"

"What on earth are we doing here?" interrupted Sebastian.

"To say the least," she admitted. "But I know that exfiltration, especially in this decisive moment of deception, would dangerously undermine the entire mission."

"Then, as soon as this masquerade is over," he said as they stood up to wipe wet sand off themselves. "If that invitation still stands, I'll come to North America."

"Do you trust me?" she asked while he kneeled to pick up a wildflower in the sand.

"I'm in love with you," he told her as he stuck the stem of the flower in the part of her hair wrapped behind her left ear.

"Then believe in me," she urged just before they kissed.

While they hiked a familiar, sandy trail, barefoot, all the way to the same unattractive beach hut, intense orange and red shades of sunlight brilliantly illuminated the Mediterranean Sea. Later, as the young couple affectionately held onto one another outside their remote place of residence, they felt invigorated by a collective state of determination amid the fleeting landscape, and the sunlight shimmering on the waves passing below the horizon that separated the earth's surface and sky.

Syria, Turkey, and—the Dividing Line . . .

Chapter Eighteen
Tomb of Suleyman Shah

B efore she and Sebastian were captured," said Nadia as Zahid rinsed her light brown eyes with water from a canteen that looked like the color of an olive. "Catherine hid me underneath debris."

"How long were you inside the tunnel?" asked Zahid, clad in a desert camouflage uniform, Kevlar vest, and a helmet.

"I don't know," replied the five-foot-six, thirteen-year-old, drying her eyes with part of a dark-blue hijab. "But I could hear gunfire while digging myself out,"

"All of the sand flushed out?" he asked while putting the top on the one-quart plastic canteen.

"I think so," she said, and he slipped the canteen back into the cargo pocket on his left leg.

"We're ready," Zahid told a Turkish gendarmerie kneeling on the ground next to them.

After the gendarmerie, dressed similarly to Zahid, stopped searching the corpse of a young male shot scaling down a ten-foot concrete wall on the Turkish side of the border with Syria. He stood up, slung a submachine gun around his shoulder, then signaled engineers on a demolition team. They quit loading explosive materials into several large holes intersecting a central tunnel. By then, Zahid and Nadia had taken cover behind an armored truck in a long, single-file line of other wheeled and tracked ground combat vehicles carrying more than five hundred heavily armed ODF fighters.

"Cover your ears," Zahid told Nadia as he and a leading engineer locked eyes.

With a nod of Zahid's head—an underground shock wave released tremendous subsurface pressure with the tunnel's detonation. The eruption that transformed the blast site into a vast crater also discharged blistering gases combined with sand, gravel, and clay into the atmosphere.

"Are you OK?"

"I'm fine," Nadia told him as she brushed some of the pieces of clay and sand off her green camouflage jacket and blue denim jeans. "But I'm afraid my father and brother aren't."

With a heavy heart, Zahid grabbed Nadia's hand and lowered himself to a kneeling position in front of her.

"Your father and a woman named Nina, died fighting government forces in Aleppo," he said with regret.

"My brother too?" Nadia asked with tears welling in her eyes.

"No."

"He's alive?"

"Barely," Zahid told her. "I promised your father I would continue to look after you and your brother if anything happens to him."

"Have you heard from Catherine?" Nadia asked as Turkish Air Force F-16 fighter jet engines sounded overhead. "I could tell she was in a lot of pain before she left."

"She's in stable condition with her father at Tishreen Military Hospital," replied Zahid. "But Alex and Sebastian sustained severe injuries. They're in transit with Nina's and your father's remains to the Balıklı Greek Hospital in Istanbul."

Suddenly, the engines of numerous motor vehicles started, and noisy mechanical sounds nearly created deafening conditions. To compensate, Zahid spoke louder while he continued.

"I've made arrangements with the gendarmerie for you to join Adad and Alexander in Istanbul," he explained as he stood up. "There's also a man named Gerard. You don't know him yet, but he was a good friend of your father's. Gerard has insisted on covering all of your expenses at one of Switzerland's oldest boarding schools."

"Why can't I go with you?"

"Alexander became Head of the House of Osman upon your father's death," Zahid said to her. "You retain that right if Alexander dies. As for me—I ride with the caravan."

"Where?"

"Your ancestors' tomb," Zahid explained. "The Tomb of Suleyman Shah and the forty Turkish guards protecting it are in grave danger of destruction by fighters from the Islamic State of Iraq and the Levant. That is why Turkey's president, agreeing to ODF participation in their rescue is a great honor to the House of Osman."

"Has anyone replaced my brother in ODF?"

"No."

"Then let it be me," urged Nadia as additional war-planes flew ahead of the convoy. "At least until the tomb and the guards protecting it are safe."

Sometime after that, a fierce bombardment campaign was initiated by all military aircraft connected to the oper-ation. And then, as sweet sunshine gave way to giant clouds of thick smoke billowing from exploding white phosphorus, munitions launched in support of an immi-nent ground assault. A teenage soldier showed Nadia how to operate a twenty-millimeter cannon in the bed of an old, heavy-duty, six-wheeled, five-ton desert-camouflaged truck. Meanwhile, against the backdrop of the longest river in Western Asia, the mechanized infantry unit she rode with near the Euphrates River traveled slowly—yet relentlessly closer—to where there is no freedom from liv-ing in a perpetual state of fear.

END OF TV PILOT EPISODE 101

"The Hunt for an Elusive Individual Begins."

The Old Roseans
Les Anciens Roséens

About the Author

D. Van Buren is a United States Marine Corps veteran who advocates for domestic violence awareness. A victim of unfathomable misfortune at an early age, the future author stopped talking. Later, he began binge-watching sports, movies, and cartoons, and at some point, he started speaking again. When D. Van Buren was assigned to the Marine Corps Air Ground Combat Center Twenty-Nine Palms. He became interested in creating film and television content. Besides writing, he enjoys tennis, video games, traveling, and reading. One of his favorite books is To Catch a King, written by Jack Higgins. The Old Roseans (Les Anciens Roséens) is his first publication.

> "I can do all things through Christ, which strengthens me."
>
> —Philippians 4:13